W9-AVJ-430

3 1668 05000 0007

Adrenaline burned through Cristiano's veins as he ran down the casino steps.

The cool air with its whisper of pine and the sea felt good, tasted better than the champagne he'd avoided all evening, and out in the darkness the pounding inside his head was less intense. He didn't care about anything except finding Kate Edwards.

She had gone into the Hotel de Paris when she'd run out of here. Standing in the middle of the marble floor, still reeling from the realization of who she was, he had watched her crossing the square, dodging in front of a car in her haste to get away.

He nodded curtly at the doorman, who leaped forward to open the door for him, as Suki's words came back to him. *She wasn't your type at all… Seriously plain and boring…*

She was right about the first bit, at least—Kate Edwards *was* entirely different from the women he usually bedded. And yet the experience had been worth remembering.

Worth repeating.

All about the author...
India Grey

A self-confessed romance junkie, **INDIA GREY** was just thirteen years old when she first sent off for the Harlequin® writers' guidelines. She can still recall the thrill of receiving the large brown envelope with its distinctive logo. She subsequently whiled away many a dull school day staring out the window and dreaming of the perfect hero. She kept these guidelines with her for the next ten years, tucking them carefully inside the cover of each new diary in January, and beginning every list of New Year's resolutions with the words *Start Novel*. In the meantime she also gained a degree in English literature and language from Manchester University, and in a stroke of genius on the part of the gods of romance, met her gorgeous future husband on the very last night of their three years there. The past fifteen years have been spent blissfully buried in domesticity—and heaps of pink washing generated by three small daughters—but she has never really stopped daydreaming about romance. She's just profoundly grateful to finally have an excuse to do it legitimately!

India Grey

THE SECRET SHE CAN'T HIDE

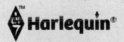

TORONTO NEW YORK LONDON
AMSTERDAM PARIS SYDNEY HAMBURG
STOCKHOLM ATHENS TOKYO MILAN MADRID
PRAGUE WARSAW BUDAPEST AUCKLAND

If you purchased this book without a cover you should be aware
that this book is stolen property. It was reported as "unsold and
destroyed" to the publisher, and neither the author nor the
publisher has received any payment for this "stripped book."

Recycling programs
for this product may
not exist in your area.

ISBN-13: 978-0-373-23761-6

THE SECRET SHE CAN'T HIDE
Previously published in the U.K. as
HER LAST NIGHT OF INNOCENCE

First North American Publication 2011

Copyright © 2010 by India Grey

All rights reserved. Except for use in any review, the reproduction or
utilization of this work in whole or in part in any form by any electronic,
mechanical or other means, now known or hereafter invented, including
xerography, photocopying and recording, or in any information storage
or retrieval system, is forbidden without the written permission of the
publisher, Harlequin Enterprises Limited, 225 Duncan Mill Road,
Don Mills, Ontario, Canada M3B 3K9.

This is a work of fiction. Names, characters, places and incidents are
either the product of the author's imagination or are used fictitiously,
and any resemblance to actual persons, living or dead, business
establishments, events or locales is entirely coincidental.

This edition published by arrangement with Harlequin Books S.A.

For questions and comments about the quality of this book
please contact us at Customer_eCare@Harlequin.ca.

® and ™ are trademarks of the publisher. Trademarks indicated with
® are registered in the United States Patent and Trademark Office, the
Canadian Trade Marks Office and in other countries.

www.eHarlequin.com

Printed in U.S.A.

THE SECRET
SHE CAN'T HIDE

To Michelle Styles,
with love and gratitude for listening,
advising and believing.

PROLOGUE

A HAZE of heat hung over the tarmac. The air was thick, acrid with the smell of hot rubber and high-octane fuel. The starting grid was thronged with reporters brandishing microphones and news crews shouldering cameras, as well as pit crews wearing overalls in their team colours and promotions girls carrying flags and wearing hardly anything at all.

Cristiano picked up his helmet and gloves and stepped out of the shade of the garages into the blazing Côte D'Azur sunlight. The noise of the crowd instantly doubled and reporters swooped, holding out their microphones to him. He kept his head down.

His body felt loose and heavy with the memory of last night's pleasure. It wasn't unusual for him to work off the residual adrenaline and testosterone from the qualifying session in the willing arms of one of the paddock club hostesses or pit lane beauties the night before a big race; sex was a good way of easing both the mental and physical tension of a Grand Prix weekend.

But last night hadn't just been sex.

'*Ciao*, Cristiano. Good of you to join us.'

Silvio Girardi, Campano team boss, came forward, perspiring heavily beneath his baseball cap as he slapped Cristiano's shoulder. A stocky, grey-haired Neapolitan, rapid-fire sarcasm was his default setting. Right now the dial was turned to maximum. 'Why you not take an extra half-hour in bed, huh? Make sure you were *really* rested for the race?'

Cristiano took a mouthful of water and grimaced. 'If I'd had an extra half-hour in bed the last thing I would have been doing is resting.'

Silvio rolled his eyes and threw his hands in the air in a gesture of elaborate exasperation. 'I hope that whichever cocktail waitress it was last night knows better than to kiss and tell. Our new sponsors were most particular that they don't want any scandal. Clearspring—it's *water*, Cristiano, not bourbon. Clean living, wholesome, for kids—*comprendo*? Did you see the guy from their marketing department yesterday?'

'It wasn't a guy.'

'Huh?' Silvio frowned. 'They said they were sending their head of marketing—a Dominic someone. You're telling me Dominic isn't a guy's name in England?'

'His wife went into labour unexpectedly. They sent his assistant.'

'A girl?'

A ghost of a smile touched Cristiano's lips as he pulled on his gloves. 'A girl.'

Oh, yes. Kate Edwards was very definitely a girl.

Nervously repositioning his baseball cap, Silvio gave a snort of contempt. 'Well, I hope you were nice to her—no funny business. I need the money. You get paid millions just for showing up and sitting in a car it costs me millions to build for you. Think about it—how is this fair?' He was pacing around the low emerald-green car with its Clearspring banners. 'Now—time for you to do some work and show what this beauty can do. You're in pole position. You can't lose.'

With another slap on the back, he moved off to talk to the mechanics and engineers. Cristiano turned round, combing the crowd for a honey-coloured head amongst the peroxide blondes and polished brunettes.

Slim, brown arms twined around his neck, and he was enveloped in a familiar musky perfume.

'Good luck,' his PA whispered huskily in his ear.

Fighting irritation, he pulled away and looked over her shoulder. 'Thanks, Suki.'

Where was Kate?

'How was the interview yesterday evening with the girl from Clearspring? I hope it didn't drag on too long. She looked a little bit…' Suki's glossy lips twitched into a smirk '…serious.'

'It was fine.' As far as he was concerned, it hadn't dragged on nearly long enough. 'Have you seen her?'

Suki raised one dark, perfectly arched brow. 'This morning? Why would I have? Is she here?'

'*Si.*' Cristiano's gaze moved restlessly over the PR girls, posing and pouting for the cameras in their team colours, and the journalists jostling for last-minute interviews. The excitement of the crowds of people packed into the grandstands and on every balcony and rooftop overlooking the street circuit was reaching fever-pitch, and the yachts sounded their horns plaintively out in Monaco harbour.

Suki shrugged her narrow shoulders in the tight-fitting Campano T-shirt. 'Well, if I see her I'll tell her you said hi,' she said coolly. 'But it's pretty much time for you to get in the car.'

For a second he looked at her blankly, as if what she was saying meant nothing to him. Then he shook his head curtly. 'I know.'

He turned away, thrusting his hands into his hair, gritting his teeth against a sudden urge to walk away, tear off his overalls and keep walking until he found her.

The television crew who had been talking to the team next to him on the grid finished their interview and began to head in his direction. Cristiano felt black despair pulling at him. The seconds were ticking away, and he could hear the crowd chanting his name. It was too late.

And then he saw her.

She was standing in the middle of the milling hordes of people in the pit lane, looking around. Her head was turned away from him, her face obscured for a moment by the curtain of her dark-blonde hair, but there was no mistaking the length of her legs in the faded jeans she wore, the swell of those breasts beneath the navy T-shirt she'd picked up that morning from his bedroom floor.

He was smiling as he walked towards her, wondering how he could have missed her. Amidst all the painted pedigree grid-girls, she looked like an abandoned golden retriever puppy. He'd noticed her as soon as he had pulled into the pit lane after qualifying yesterday, because she was so different from the standard Grand Prix girl groupies. In her businesslike grey suit, with her hair pulled back, she'd reminded him of the clever girls at school. The ones who'd always had clean, neat uniforms and who had done their homework on time and been held up as a shining example by the nuns.

Instead of being a waster. A no-hoper. Like him.

'Oh...'

She turned then, her full lips parting in a gasp of surprise and relief as he took her hand and dragged her into the shadow of the pit lane garages.

Kate felt heat explode inside her, spreading upwards to her cheeks and downwards to her knickers. 'I couldn't find you,' she said a little breathlessly, ducking her head and leaning it against his chest as he pulled her into his body, hiding her fiery blush.

'I'm here.'

'I was beginning to think that I'd imagined it all.'

Oh, God—did that make her sound needy? Desperate? She laughed, but there was a slight break in it. 'Or that it had all been a dream.'

'Which bit of it would you like me to reassure you was real…?' He lowered his head and spoke lazily into her hair, his husky voice with its outrageously sensual Italian accent sending shivers of bliss down her spine as his hands gripped her waist. 'The bit in the swimming pool…or the bit in the bedroom? The kitchen floor this morning…?'

'Shh…' She was laughing, gripping the edges of his racing overalls with their Clearspring logos, her face buried in his chest. 'Someone might hear.'

'Would that be so bad?'

The laughter died and her smile faded. 'It's not my usual style.' That had to be a strong contender in the 'Understatement of the Year' competition. 'We only met yesterday—I came to *interview* you…'

'And to think I've always hated interviews,' he drawled softly. 'I'd have agreed to do more if I knew they could be so much fun.'

Kate frowned. 'I hardly know you.'

He took her chin between his fingers and tilted her head up so she had no choice but to look into those dark, bitter-chocolate coloured eyes. Famous eyes, familiar to her from television and magazines, from the countless photographs they had of him in the office, the poster on her younger brother's bedroom wall…

'After last night you know me better than anyone.'

His tone was ironic, but his swarthy pirate's face with its high, hard cheekbones and finely shaped mouth was suddenly bleak. He shook his head slowly, thrusting a hand through his dark, deliciously untidy hair. '*Gesu*, Kate, I've never…bared my soul like that before.'

'Me neither.'

Kate's voice was just a whisper as her mind flickered back over the last twelve extraordinary hours. There had been the sex, of course, and that had been…*magical*. But they had also talked. Her heart contracted painfully and her breath hitched in her throat as she remembered how he'd lain in her arms, his voice oddly toneless as he told her about his past, the difficulties he had experienced in school that had driven him to seek success at all costs. And he had seen past the professional veneer she'd so painstakingly constructed to the secret void of grief and terror beneath. He'd told her that a life lived in fear was no life at all. And he'd shown her how to shut off the anxiety and live for the moment…

From outside the garages the noise of the crowd seemed to swell in the heat, pressing against the fragile walls of their private world. He pulled away from her, his expression suddenly blank.

'I have to go.'

Kate nodded quickly and took a step back, desperate not to appear needy. 'I know. Go. But remember— you don't have to prove *anything*, Cristiano.' She managed a crooked smile. 'Drive carefully.'

For a heartbeat she saw a flicker of pain in his eyes, and then it was gone, and he was pulling on his gloves, giving her that wry, mocking smile that turned her inside out. '*Tesoro*, this is the Monaco Grand Prix. Driving carefully isn't really the idea.'

She laughed, pushing back the panic that swelled inside her. 'OK, fair point.' She wasn't going to be that person anymore—he had shown her how to live for the moment, to seize happiness, not to cling to fear. Even so, as he turned to go it took a massive effort to keep the smile in place and not let him see how this terrified her.

He was at the mouth of the garage now. Catching a glimpse of him, the crowd outside had begun to roar again. He turned, looking at her for a moment with dark, opaque eyes.

'This isn't over, you know. Last night was just the beginning.' He smiled briefly. 'Wait for me.'

And then he was gone, striding out into the shimmering haze of heat and petrol, his broad shoulders very straight. A stranger again.

The click of the harness was the signal Cristiano used mentally to switch off the outside world. From that moment there was nothing but the track, the car, the race.

He was first on the grid. The Monaco circuit was ridiculously narrow, making overtaking almost impossible, and the crowd was so close that at times you could count the gold fillings in the teeth of the billionaires on their yachts, and read the labels on the designer bikinis of their mistresses and trophy wives.

The first few laps melted away. Coming into the Grand Hotel Hairpin on the fourth—or was it the fifth?—a good half-second ahead of the competition, Cristiano changed gear smoothly, allowing his mind to pan out a little from its minute focus on the track. Silvio had done well. The car was performing perfectly. The conditions were ideal. The race was his—another win to add to his impressive record.

You don't have to prove anything...

Darkness engulfed him as he plunged into the tunnel. The soft voice in his head was so real that for a moment it was as if she was in the car with him, and he could almost smell the cool scent of her skin. His focus wavered and he blinked hard, almost dizzy with longing.

The mouth of the tunnel was ahead of him. As he came out the sun was in his eyes, the taste of her skin was on his lips, the echo of her words in his ears, and suddenly he had the oddest sensation of everything making sense. The barrier in front of him was too close, coming too fast, but it felt almost unreal because in that moment he *knew*...

And then there was an explosion—pain, fire, blackness.

Nothing.

CHAPTER ONE

Four years later

CLEARSPRING WATER, as the marketing department was keen to point out, was sourced from an ancient spring deep in the green heart of the Yorkshire Dales. Its offices, however, were situated in a hideous 1960s building on an industrial estate on the fringes of a grey Yorkshire town.

They were pretty depressing at the best of times, but on the first Monday morning in January the drooping paper chains and balding Christmas tree in Reception that no one had quite got round to removing made them feel more than usually grim. Standing in the cell-like kitchen at the end of the corridor, waiting for the kettle to boil, Kate stared at the calendar on the wall in front of her.

New year, new calendar. New set of photographs of the Campano racing team.

Pulling the sleeves of the rather unflattering polo-necked jumper her mother had given her for Christmas down over her fingers, she turned her back on the calendar and leaned against the worktop, repeating her New Year's resolution in her head like a mantra. *This year I am going to stop waiting. I am going to give up dealing in maybes and what ifs; stop obsessing over what I haven't got, and make the most of what I have—a gorgeous, happy, healthy three-year-old boy.*

Her fingers tingled. She wasn't going to look. Wasn't going to pull the stupid calendar off the wall and flick through in search of a photo of Cristiano Maresca like some obsessed teenage fangirl.

As she had last year. And the one before.

Cristiano Maresca hadn't raced since the accident that had almost killed him at Monaco, but if anything his status as a celebrity heart-throb had only increased. He was more elusive than ever, but rare snatched paparazzi photographs of him looking lean and menacing were reproduced endlessly in newspapers and magazines, along with speculation about whether he'd ever return to the circuit.

Why was the kettle taking so long to boil?

She took down mugs from the cupboard, threw a herbal teabag into the one that said 'The Boss' on it, and spooned coffee into 'I'd rather be in Tenerife'. The kettle was just beginning the throaty splutter that was a prelude to its great crescendo as it reached boiling point. Kate's gaze flickered back to the calendar.

January's photo was harmless enough, showing two of the Campano cars—Clearspring banners clearly visible—racing side by side. Surreptitiously, as if it had a mind of its own, she felt her hand come up, lifting the page so she could see the picture underneath.

'July.'

The voice from behind her made her jump. Kate snatched her hand back as Lisa from the art department stuck her head round the door.

'Don't pretend you weren't looking for Maresca.' She grinned. 'We all have. He's July. Roll on summer!'

The kettle reached its final death rattle in a billowing cloud of steam as Lisa disappeared down the corridor. Grimly, Kate sloshed water into the mugs and followed, allowing herself a brief moment of triumph as she knocked on the door of Dominic's office.

She hadn't looked, and she had until July to get her life together and move on. Or give up coffee.

'What the hell is that?' Dominic peered suspiciously into the mug as she set it down on his desk and then gave a groan. 'Oh, God—it's a conspiracy. Don't tell me Lizzie's got you on board with this appalling New Year detox idea?'

Kate raised an eyebrow. 'Happy New Year to you too,' she said sardonically, turning and heading back towards the door. 'And you're welcome.'

'Wait—sorry,' Dominic sighed. 'A whole week in the company of my mother-in-law seems to have brought out my petulant side. Let me try that again, in the manner of a civilised human being who is delighted to be back at work at the start of an exciting new year.' He beamed comically, gesturing to the chair squeezed into the gap between the window and the filing cabinet opposite his desk. 'Have a seat and tell me about your Christmas. I take it you weren't buried beneath an avalanche of pink plastic like we were?'

Cupping her coffee in both hands, Kate sat down. Nine months older than her son, Dominic's daughter Ruby was both Alexander's best friend and his nemesis. Between them, they seemed to have dedicated their lives to proving any child psychologist who claimed that gender roles weren't programmed from birth an idiot.

'Nope, it was wall-to-wall cars with us,' Kate said ruefully. 'Alexander's favourite by miles is the Alfa Romeo whatever-it-was from you.' She took a sip of coffee. 'He even takes it to bed with him. Thank you.'

'My pleasure,' Dominic said with a wistful sigh. 'It's a Spider, you hopeless girl. An Alfa Romeo Spider—and Alexander's quite right. It's one of the most iconic cars ever made. I'd go to bed with one if I could.'

'Does Lizzie know about this?'

'I'm sure she wouldn't be surprised,' Dominic said wryly, putting down his mug with a little grimace of distaste. 'An Alfa Romeo Spider would never make me go on a detox programme.'

'Serves you right. You shouldn't have partied so hard over Christmas.'

Dominic leaned back in his chair. 'Yes, well, you know what this job's like. Clients to entertain, staff parties to organise.' He looked at her pointedly over his glasses. 'Even though some staff didn't bother to turn up.'

Kate rolled her eyes, suddenly taking a great interest in rearranging the Post-it notes stuck all over the filing cabinet into tidy lines. 'Come on, we've been through this before. I couldn't get a babysitter, OK?'

'Your mum was out clubbing again, was she?'

The unlikeliness of the image made Kate smile briefly in spite of herself. 'I can't ask her all the time. She already does enough, looking after Alexander for me when I'm working. It's not as if I can afford to pay her or anything.'

'She wouldn't take it even if you could. You know she loves having him. It's been a lifeline for her after Will…'

'I know, I know.' Kate pressed her finger down on the corner of a Post-it note that stubbornly refused to stick. 'Having a little boy around again takes her back to happier times, I guess, when both Will and my dad were alive. But I still don't like to rely on her too much. I got myself into this situation, and as far as possible it's up to me to deal with it on my own.'

Dominic took another unenthusiastic sip of herbal tea. 'You didn't get into it entirely on your own,' he observed dryly. 'Not unless it was an immaculate conception.'

It was pretty perfect, Kate thought bleakly, staring out over the grey, rain-soaked car park and thinking of a warm swimming pool, a quiet pine-and-lavender-scented night. But then she hadn't had anything to compare it to—before or since—and, given that she hadn't been out for an evening without Alexander in over six months, that wasn't likely to change any time soon. She really must buy some decent clothes and go out with Lisa and the other girls next time they invited her. If they hadn't given up asking her.

'Hell-*lo*?' Dominic's voice, sounding distinctly tetchy, cut through her thoughts. 'Are you listening to a word I'm saying?'

'Sorry,' she muttered, dragging her gaze away from the car park and her attention back to Dominic. 'Immaculate conception. Getting into this on my own.'

Dominic sighed. Leaning forward, he put his elbows on the desk, rubbing his hands over his face and pushing his glasses up. 'That's the point—you didn't get into it on your own, and you shouldn't have to deal with it on your own either. Parenting is bloody hard work. It takes two people to make a baby for a very good reason.'

Kate's heart sank as it began to dawn on her that Dominic was steering this conversation in a specific direction, and it wasn't one that Kate wanted to go in. 'I'm doing my best,' she said defensively. 'I know it's not ideal, believe me, but I'm doing all I—'

'I'm not saying you're not,' Dominic interrupted gently. 'You're a fantastic mother.'

Kate put her mug down carefully on the desk. Her heart had started to beat a little faster, and she had an odd sensation, as if something cold and heavy was pressing on her chest.

'But?'

'It's been four years, Kate, and you're still holding on—hoping that a tall, dark Italian racing driver is going to come roaring down the high street and pull you into his arms.'

Kate got to her feet with a bright smile. 'OK—coffee break over. I'd love to stay and chat, but I have a load of work to do on the Healthy Schools account, so if you'll—'

'I'm sorry, I'm sorry.' Dominic had got up too, his hands held up in a gesture of surrender, although he had also moved to one side of his desk so that he was effectively blocking her exit. 'I'm not handling this very well, am I? Lizzie and I are worried about you, that's all. The Christmas party was the last in a long list of Kate no-shows, and it just seems like you've been frozen in the same place for too long.'

Kate really didn't want to ask, but couldn't see that she had much choice. 'What place?'

Dominic met her eyes steadily, giving her the distinct impression that he was preparing himself to say something he'd been planning for a while. 'You're still waiting for a man you don't really believe is ever going to show up, and yet you can't quite bear to stop hoping.'

She turned her head away sharply, so that he wouldn't see the pain on her face as Cristiano's words came back to her.

This isn't over, you know. Last night was just the beginning. Wait for me.

'Ah, well,' she said with quiet bitterness, 'that's where you're wrong. It's my New Year's resolution to do exactly that.'

'And how well did you do with that one last year?' Dominic joked and then, sensing her anguish, softened his tone. 'The problem is, you're not going to be able to do it while everything is so unresolved. You need closure. You need to know once and for all that things are over between you, and I don't think that'll happen until you've told him that he has a son.'

Kate had stayed standing in the hope that she could wind this conversation up quickly and be on her way, but suddenly she wasn't sure that was going to be possible. Or that it was turning out to be the kind of conversation that she could have without sitting down.

'Not this again, Dominic. I tried that, remember?' She sank back onto the chair and looked down at her hands. 'Twice.'

'I know you did, lovey, but you don't actually know that the message got through. You wrote to him. But letters go astray—fall into the wrong hands. I think that for Alexander's sake you have to try again. In a way that leaves no room for doubt.'

In her lap Kate's fingers were twisted together, the bones showing white beneath the roughened, winter-dry skin. 'I'm not interested in trapping him,' she said, very quietly. 'I really don't want to *force* him into acknowledging me, or Alexander.'

'But it's his *responsibility.*'

There was a hint of exasperation in Dominic's tone now, though he was doing his best to hide it. Oddly, it strengthened Kate's resolve.

'I don't care,' she said firmly. 'I don't *need* Cristiano's help—Alexander and I are fine on our own. Finding out I was pregnant was such a massive shock at the beginning, especially coming on top of the accident and everything, but I'm so glad it happened now. I love Alexander more than I could ever have thought possible.' She hesitated for a second, swallowing the lump of emotion that had suddenly formed in her throat. 'I know it would be better if he had a father—for him and for me—but only if he wanted to be there.'

Dominic turned and chucked the remainder of his herbal tea into the pot of a sickly-looking yukka behind his desk. 'You don't know for sure that he doesn't.'

'Oh, I think I do.' Kate gave a dry, humourless laugh, turning her empty mug between her hands as if trying to absorb some of its fading warmth. 'He did actually tell me that he didn't want children when

I interviewed him, so it was hardly a surprise when he didn't answer my letters. But I did try to see him as well, don't forget. I stood for two days outside the hospital, with the hardcore press pack and a group of slightly scary fans, trying not to throw up every five minutes.'

She laughed, but tears stung at the back of her eyes as she remembered the late July heat, the constant drag of morning sickness, the growing pain and humiliation of realising she was wasting her time.

'He was in a bad way,' Dominic remarked. 'He was in a coma for ten days—those kind of injuries take some getting over.'

She flinched. The image of Cristiano, unconscious in a hospital bed was one that had haunted her during those terrible weeks. 'I *know*. But he'd been out of Intensive Care for a while then, and according to the papers he's made a full recovery. If he wanted to get in touch with me, he would have by now.'

'So where does that leave Alex?' Dominic said gruffly. 'One day he's going to want to know who his father is. He's only three years old at the moment, and already he's obsessed with cars and speed. Sooner or later...'

Kate sighed, letting go of the mug and staring down at its cheery picture of a beach and palm trees. *I really would rather be in Tenerife*, she thought wearily. 'What do you want me to do, Dominic? I tried. I wrote to him; I went to see him and couldn't get past

Security. Short of a front-page kiss-and-tell exposé in a tabloid newspaper, what else can I do?'

Wordlessly, Dominic opened the top drawer of his desk and took out a large silver envelope. He slid it across the desk towards her.

'Go and see him again.'

Kate glanced from the envelope to his face, and back down again. Her heart had started to thud uncomfortably in her chest.

'What's this?'

'An invitation.' He silently cursed himself for not sounding more casual. He took a deep breath. 'To a party at the Casino in Monte Carlo to launch the new season's Campano team…And celebrate Cristiano Maresca's return to racing.'

Kate's cornflower-blue eyes widened, seeking out his and seeming to search them from a face that was suddenly the same colour as the pale grey sky beyond the window.

'Are you going?'

Dominic couldn't decide whether it was hope or terror that made her voice crack.

'No. I'm sending Lisa, and Ian from the Campano account. And you.'

Kate leapt to her feet, shaking her head vehemently. 'No. You can't. *I* can't. What about Alexander? I can't leave—'

Dominic had known perfectly well that this would be her main objection and was well prepared. 'He can come and stay with us—you know that he and Ruby have been pestering us for a sleepover for ages.'

Kate didn't smile. 'But I—I've never left him overnight before.'

'He'll be fine—just like Ruby was fine when she stayed with you when Lizzie and I went away for our anniversary. You're doing it for him, Kate. This is your chance to get some answers.'

'No—I can't.' She shook her head again, her hand flying to her throat, her eyes wide with fear.

Dominic felt guilt flare inside him like acid indigestion.

Losing her father in a car accident had taught six-year-old Kate Edwards that life was fragile, and that happiness and security were precarious—a lesson that had been brutally hammered home fifteen years later, when her seventeen-year-old brother had ploughed his car into a tree on the Hartley Bridge to Harrogate Road and been killed outright. Dominic had met Kate for the first time a few months after that, when he had interviewed her for a job as his assistant at Clearspring.

She had come back to stay in Hartley Bridge and be near her mother after university, she'd explained. It had been obvious within five minutes that she was capable of doing the job with her eyes closed, but also that she was a girl who was holding herself together by the skin of her teeth. He'd given her the job, and over the next year had watched the anxiety begin to fade from her eyes as her confidence grew.

She'd been the obvious person to go to Monaco in his place when Ruby had made her unexpectedly early appearance, and he'd hoped that the trip would do her good—show her that there was a whole world beyond Hartley Bridge, and that aeroplanes were convenient methods of transport rather than plot devices in disaster movies.

It had all backfired spectacularly, leaving Kate more aware than ever of the risk involved in reaching for happiness. Hence Dominic's guilt, and his feeling of responsibility to both her and Alexander. Sitting on the sofa with a bottle of wine the other night, he and Lizzie had decided that the Campano party was an opportunity to break the cycle once and for all. Tough love. That was what they'd called it.

Now it just felt cruel.

'What's the worst that could happen?' he asked gently.

Looking out over the dingy car park, her eyes were huge in her pale face. 'For once, I don't even know where to begin to answer that,' she said with a brave attempt at a laugh. 'What if he doesn't remember me? What if I got it totally wrong and to him I was just another anonymous, meaningless one-night stand? What if he's there, surrounded by beautiful, adoring women, and he completely blanks me?'

'Then it's his loss.' Dominic sighed. His caffeine craving was starting to bite, and this was the kind of conversation Lizzie was so much better at. 'And you'll know he was never worthy of your heart, or the time you've spent waiting for him, and you can finally move on.'

'And Alexander?'

'Look—here's what I suggest.' Frowning, Dominic got to his feet and shoved his hands into his pockets in what every member of the Clearspring marketing department would recognise as an indication that he meant business. 'I think you should write Cristiano a letter, containing the basic facts about Alexander's birth and leaving the name of your solicitor where he can contact you. If he doesn't acknowledge you at the party, you can leave it with a member of his staff and come home knowing that this time you really have done all you can.'

Stunned into a moment's silence, Kate blinked. 'You've thought it all through, haven't you?'

'I've thought of nothing else since this damned invitation arrived.'

'I haven't got anything to wear.'

Despite her defensively tensed shoulders, Dominic recognised the final protest of a woman who knew she was defeated. He felt a small glow of tentative triumph.

'So buy something. I'll look after the kids at the weekend, and you and Lizzie can hit the shops in Leeds.'

'I can't afford it,' Kate protested weakly. 'I'm a single parent, remember?'

Reaching into the drawer again, Dominic took out his chequebook and began to scribble. Tearing it out, he handed a cheque to her with a grin. 'Take this and buy something stunning, and hopefully you won't be for much longer.'

'It's going to be quite a party.'

Dr Francine Fournier looked up from the invitation in her hand and raised a perfectly shaped, brutally eloquent eyebrow. 'I'm just sorry I can't be there, but unfortunately tonight is—'

'Please—there's no need to explain.' Cristiano got up from the chair and walked a few paces across the thick carpet of Dr Fournier's consulting room before turning back to her with a bleak smile. 'I think we both know that the whole thing is a complete sham. I wouldn't be going myself if I had any choice.'

Outside, the February dusk was falling early over Nice, and a thin slick of rain made the pavements glisten. In here, the lamps cast a soft glow over serious seascapes in oil, and a huge bowl of white hyacinths on the desk perfumed the centrally heated air. There was nothing remotely clinical about the room apart from the lightbox on the wall with its illuminated display of cross-sections of Cristiano's brain.

Dr Fournier sighed, slipping the invitation inside the cover of the file of notes that lay open on the desk in front of her. 'It's not a sham, Cristiano,' she said, in the grave, low-pitched voice she used for breaking bad news to families. 'It's just a little premature, perhaps.'

'Premature?' Cristiano echoed hollowly, thrusting

his balled fists into his pockets and walking over to look more closely at the X-ray images, as if he might be able to see something in the intricate whorls and dark spaces that Dr Fournier had missed. 'By how long? A year? A decade? A lifetime? Because, from what you've just told me, I'm never going to be able to race again.'

Francine Fournier was forty-eight years old, and had been happily married to her second husband for six years. She was also one of Europe's most senior and well-respected brain injury specialists, but, in spite of all these things, she still had to steel herself against the spark of attraction as she looked from the images of the inside of Cristiano Maresca's head to the face of the man himself.

'I didn't say that.'

The light from the X-ray box emphasised his pallor, and the lines of tension etched around his impossibly sexy mouth, but neither of those things detracted from his extraordinary good-looks.

'Not in so many words,' he said hoarsely. 'But if you can't find out what's wrong with me and work out how to put it right, it amounts to the same thing.'

'It's not that simple, Cristiano. The good news is that you're looking at a healthy brain. Those X-rays show that your recovery from the accident has been remarkably complete.' She picked up the top sheet from the file and frowned slightly as she studied it. 'All your stats are excellent—proving that your re-flexes and responses far exceed those of the average fit male your age. My investigations have been exhaustive, and I can state categorically that there's no *physiological* cause of the symptoms you've been having.'

He gave a hollow laugh. 'You're saying that it's all in my mind?'

'The brain is a very complex organ. Physical injury is easy to see, but psychological damage is harder to measure. The palpitations and flashbacks you're suffering while driving are very real symptoms, but their cause is nothing I can specifically identify or treat.' She paused, rearranging the papers on her desk, her large diamond eternity ring flashing in the lamplight as her hands moved. 'I believe,' she began again carefully, 'that they are directly related to your memory loss. In itself, that's not a problem, but because your subconscious has blocked out memories of the crash you haven't yet been able to process them and move on.'

'But what about *before* the crash?' Cristiano's voice was like sandpaper. 'Why can't I remember that either?'

'Retrograde amnesia,' Dr Fournier said gently. 'It's not uncommon. Many people experience some degree of memory loss after a head trauma. The length of time that's lost is significant—the fact that you've only got a gap of twenty-four hours is good news.'

Cristiano gave a hard, abrupt laugh. 'Is it?' Silhouetted against the gathering darkness outside, his broad shoulders were absolutely rigid. 'Will I ever get them back?'

'It's impossible to say. There are no guarantees. Sometimes memory comes back in its own time.'

He swore in Italian, softly and savagely. 'I can't wait for that. The Grand Prix season starts in six weeks.' Thrusting a hand through his hair, he gave a ragged, bitter laugh. 'Suki's invited every sports journalist and team sponsor on the planet to this ridiculous event tonight to celebrate my return to the circuit. Silvio has rediscovered religion thanks to the miracle of my recovery.'

Dr Fournier's voice was deliberately soothing. 'Have you talked to the people you were with that night? Sometimes you just need a trigger for the memory to return…'

Cristiano gave an impatient shake of his head. 'I was alone. The last thing I remember is getting into the car for qualifying.' He had been over it time and time again. He remembered the click of the harness as he'd got into the car, and after that nothing. Sometimes, just as he was drifting off to sleep or waking up again, he thought he caught the echo of something that was a memory rather than a dream, and desperately tried to hold onto it, but the harder he tried the more elusive it was. 'Suki tells me I did an interview with someone from Clearspring Water, but that can't have taken long. After that I must have gone home.'

Leaning against the windowsill, he dropped his

head into his hands for a moment as despair and self-disgust overwhelmed him. Against the odds he had survived a crash that should have killed him, come round from ten days in a coma and dragged himself from an Intensive Care bed back to the cockpit of a racing car. He had built up his strength, and driven himself ruthlessly and relentlessly to regain fitness, harnessing the same determination and focus that had made him so successful before.

Now everything he had worked for was slipping through his fingers. And there was nothing he could do about it—because while he could control his body and work harder, train longer, push himself further, his brain still let him down.

'Don't forget that you are lucky to have survived, Cristiano.'

He raised his head and looked at the doctor with an expression of infinite despair. 'If I can't race again, I might as well not have.'

Dr Fournier tapped her finger thoughtfully against her compressed lips. 'When was the last time you had a holiday?'

He shrugged. 'Relaxing has never really been my thing.'

'Maybe you should try it. You've pushed yourself as far as you possibly can physically, so maybe now it's time to give yourself a rest. Take some time out to think.'

'No thanks.'

He had spent his life trying to avoid having time to

think. Escaping from introspection had always been one of the driving forces behind everything he did.

Dr Fournier shrugged one cashmere shoulder. 'It's the best shot you've got of getting your memory back. Since you left hospital you haven't stopped pushing yourself—almost as if you have to prove to yourself that you're not just as fit as you were before the accident, but fitter, stronger, better. You've done it, Cristiano—congratulations. Physically, you're in peak condition. However, mentally...'

'Thank you, Doctor.' He gave her a glacial smile. 'You don't need to remind me about my mental failings.'

'Needing time to get over a trauma like you've had isn't a failing—and I'm not saying this as your doctor; I'm saying it as your friend. I have a chalet in the Alps, near Courchevel. It's pretty isolated, but a housekeeper keeps it stocked up with the essentials and the skiing is great.' She opened the top drawer of her desk and took out a set of keys. They gave a silvery jangle as she held them out to him across the desk, looking at him steadily. 'It's yours for as long as you want it.'

And, because he had run out of options, because he was desperate, because it was the only glimmer of hope left on an increasingly dark horizon, Cristiano found himself leaning forward and taking them from her.

'Go, Cristiano,' she said gravely. 'Go soon.'

CHAPTER TWO

'OMIGOD—you will never *guess* who's just arriving...'

Kate jerked her head up, almost stabbing herself with the mascara wand, as Lisa's shriek of excitement ricocheted off her taut nerves.

'OK, tell me.'

Lisa, already dressed and ready to go in a skin-tight silver dress that showed off her magnificent figure to perfection, was stationed at the French windows looking out over the front of the hotel to where the Monaco Casino lit up the night like an elegant ocean liner. The guests for the Campano party were already arriving: a steady procession of shiny, sporty, expensive cars pulling up in front of the Casino's famous Belle Epoque frontage to disgorge their glamorous occupants while Lisa gave an increasingly excited commentary.

'Oh...no, wait a minute...it isn't,' she said now, her voice suddenly flat with disappointment. 'I thought it was Maresca, but it's not...Too short...'

In the mirror, Kate's own eyes stared back at her—wide, and dark with terror as well as with unfamiliar make-up. Just the mention of his name and her hands, already shaking enough to make putting on mascara a very hazardous exercise, were damp and slick with sweat. Why had she ever thought she could actually go through with this?

Letting the curtain drop back into place, Lisa peeled herself away from her vantage point and picked up her mini-bar vodka and tonic. Taking a sip, she almost spat it out again as Kate turned round.

'Wow—just look at you!' she squealed, peering at Kate through thick false eyelashes as she came forward. 'Who the hell would have thought that you'd scrub up like that, Miss Edwards?' She circled around Kate and came back to stand in front of her, an expression of such astonished admiration on her face that Kate wasn't sure whether she should be flattered or insulted. 'The dress is fabulous. Fab. *U*. Lous. And where have you been hiding that figure?'

'The dress was Lizzie's choice,' Kate muttered, tugging it over her straining cleavage. 'There's absolutely no way I would have gone for anything so revealing. You don't think it's too much, do you?'

As she asked the question she realised that since Lisa was wearing thigh-skimming silver sequins teamed with vertiginous over-the-knee black patent platform boots, her idea of 'too much' might not be completely reliable.

'Absolutely not.' Lisa's eyes skimmed over Kate, taking in every detail of the midnight-blue satin dress, with its plunging halter-neck and gathered pleats held in a diamond clasp nestling between her breasts. She shook her head. 'You are a dark horse, you know. I always thought there might be hidden depths behind that Plain Jane exterior you present in the office.'

Kate moved away, letting her hair fall over her face as she bent to slip on the impossibly high-heeled and pointy-toed shoes Lizzie had made her buy. 'Oh, I'm completely not. I'm one of the most boring and straightforward people in the world—seriously.'

Lisa wandered over to the mirror, leaning forward and checking her own cleavage before pouting her glossed lips thoughtfully. 'I was really surprised when I heard you were coming on this trip, since you don't even work on the Campano account any more. I suppose it's because you came out here all those years ago and did that interview with Maresca, isn't it?'

Kate felt sick. 'Yes, I suppose so. Now, what do we need—invitation, hotel key, money…?'

'Apparently there's going to be poker and roulette,' Lisa said, her butterfly mind mercifully alighting on a new subject as she sprayed on more perfume. 'Just like in a James Bond film. I've always fancied having a go at all that. What about you—are you going to get down to some serious gambling tonight?'

Kate had to reach out and lean against the edge of the bed for support as a black wave of panic swept over her, catching her off guard.

'Yes.'

It came out as a kind of odd, breathless gasp, and

she had to pretend to be adjusting the heel of her shoe as she doubled up against the pain.

At that moment there was a loud volley of knocks on the door. Lisa checked the time on her phone as she chucked it into her tiny silver clutch bag and crossed the room to open it. 'That'll be Ian. I said we'd meet him in the bar at seven-thirty, and that was fifteen minutes ago. He must have come to see what's keeping us. OK! I'm coming!' she yelled as the hammering started up again.

'You go,' Kate called after her. 'I'm ready, but I just want to phone and say goodnight to Alexander. Please—you two go ahead. I'll come over when I'm done.'

'OK, if you're sure,' Lisa said, clearly recoiling from the idea of putting her evening on hold for something as boring as phoning home to speak to a three-year-old. 'We'll see you in there. Unless, of course, I've been swept off my feet and taken into a dark alcove by Cristiano Maresca before you get there...'

The door slammed behind her. Sinking down onto the bed, Kate listened to her laughter fading as she and Ian walked away down the corridor. She squeezed her eyes shut and let out a shaky breath.

Suddenly it was very quiet.

Since they'd got to Leeds airport at two o'clock that afternoon Lisa had kept up a constant stream of chatter that had almost driven Kate demented, but it had also provided a very useful distraction from the spiralling vortex of her own fears. Now they all came rushing in to fill the silence.

With a shaking hand she picked up her phone, longing to hear Alexander's voice. Maybe that would remind her what she was doing this for. And stop her from packing her bags and getting in a taxi back to the airport.

Standing in front of the mirror, Cristiano dropped the ends of the silk bow tie for the sixth time and swore viciously.

No matter how many formal awards dinners and black tie sports events he'd attended over the years it had never got any easier. It was as if the ridiculous thing had a mind of its own and was determined to show him up as an impostor—a boy from the back alleys of Naples. The boy in the second-hand school blazer, who couldn't write a line in an exercise book without smudging the ink or letting the words slide all over the page. The boy who would never amount to anything.

Damn.

Above the upturned white collar of his shirt, a muscle jumped in his freshly shaven cheek as his old friend despair wrapped him in its suffocating embrace. Damn Suki for coming up with the idea of this absurd and completely inappropriate party.

Damn *him* for going along with it.

Turning away from the mirror, he thrust his hands through hair that was still damp from the shower and exhaled heavily. Pretty much everything he'd achieved in the last twelve years had been as a result of his need to escape his past, but he had always shied away from looking too far into the future. There was no point. His future had always looked dazzlingly assured, so he'd lived in the moment, putting all his energy and his focus into making the most of *now*.

Death or glory. Those had always seemed to be the potential outcomes for his life. He'd either keep winning until he was ready to stop, or die in a ball of flame. This struggle with demons he couldn't see, didn't understand, had never occurred to him as a possibility.

Yanking the tie from round his neck he tossed it onto the bed and walked across the expanse of gleaming wooden floor to the wardrobe—the only other piece of furniture in the huge room. He'd bought the Art Deco villa high in the hills above Monte Carlo six years ago now, but had somehow never got round to furnishing it properly. In the old days before his accident, he had simply been too busy—travelling around the Grand Prix circuits in the summer months, away skiing or scuba diving or training out of season. And since the crash...

Viciously he slid back the wardrobe door and dragged out the battered leather holdall that had accompanied him around the racetracks of the world. Since the crash it had been as if he was waiting, he acknowledged bleakly. Waiting for a thousand bits of jigsaw to fit back together again before he moved on with his life.

Except now it was obvious that it wasn't going to happen like that, because some of the bits were missing.

Maybe now it's time to give yourself a rest. Take some time out to think. It's the best shot you've got…

Dr Fournier's voice echoed inside his head as he pulled clothes from the shelves in the wardrobe, shoving them into the holdall. He was used to packing light and packing quickly, and it took him only a couple of minutes to get together all the things he needed and throw the keys to the chalet on the top. At the first opportunity he was going to get the hell out of the party and drive up to Courchevel.

As he zipped up the bag he allowed himself a twisted smile. For once in his life he was going to do as he was told. Because he intended to beat this memory loss and start winning again.

Whatever it took.

''Night, Mummy.'

'Goodnight, darling. Sweet dreams… I'll phone again in the—'

There was a muffled click and then a high-pitched tone that told her that Alexander had hung up already. He'd sounded in great spirits, and although she wasn't confident he and Ruby would be asleep any time soon, she wasn't worried about him being miserable either.

That was just her.

She listened to the tone for a few seconds more, unwilling to sever the tenuous connection that had for a few minutes stretched across all the dark miles that separated them. Then with massive effort she pressed the button, tossed her phone into her black velvet evening bag and stood up. Her face in the brightly lit hotel mirror was ghostly pale. Her eyes—by contrast—were enormous and glittering feverishly. Her hair, newly washed, hung loose around her face to her shoulders, kinking horribly because it had dried long before Lisa had finished hogging the hairdryer. Lizzie had shown her how to coil it up and pin it into one of those sexy, wispy styles that other women always seemed so good at, but when Kate had tried earlier her hands had been shaking so much she'd had to give up. Oh, well, it was good to have something to hide behind anyway.

She carefully applied the dark red lipstick Lizzie had made her buy at outrageous expense in the cosmetics hall of Harvey Nichols, and stood back to look at the effect. Oh, God, she had just gone from ghostly to vampire. Dead to undead, she thought, reaching for a tissue and scrubbing it off again. It was no good. Lizzie might have lectured her endlessly on the need to make the most of herself and stand out from the crowd, to maximise the chance of Cristiano Maresca noticing her, but it really wasn't her.

And last time he'd seen past the terrible prim grey suit and noticed her. No make-up, no cleavage-displaying dress, no killer heels. He'd seen her—the real her—with all her dark fears and anxiety that she spent her whole life trying to hide. And he'd talked to her too, telling her things about himself and his past that had made her heart turn over.

Gesu, Kate, I've never...bared my soul like that before.

And that, thought Kate bleakly, pulling open the door and going out into the corridor, was why she had spent the last four years waiting for him. Because when he had told her those things a link had been forged between them that went deeper than the physical. Before she'd met him she'd had so many misconceptions and prejudices about him, and what he did for a living, but he had smashed them all to pieces and let her see the truth.

She got into the lift, trying not to look at her reflection in its mirrored interior in case the longing that was suddenly raging inside her was written all over her face. She mustn't allow herself to get her hopes up. She had enough to lose tonight without adding her dignity and her composure to the long list.

Alexander, for example.

'*Bonsoir, mademoiselle.*' The young doorman stood aside for her with a flourish, and a blast of icy air made her shiver. 'Can I get you a taxi?'

'No, thank you,' she murmured, looking across the square to where the Casino's twin turrets pointed upwards at the inky sky. 'I'm just going... over there.'

'To the Campano party? *Bien, mademoiselle.* Enjoy your evening.'

That, thought Kate, going carefully down the steps of the hotel in her high-heeled shoes, was extremely unlikely. But then, she hadn't come here to enjoy herself. She'd come here for closure.

The square was quieter now. The party inside the Casino had already started, and the photographers Lisa had watched gathering around the entrance earlier, to capture the arrival of celebrities and sports personalities, had dispersed, leaving only a few ambling, curious tourists. Blue lights from the Casino's entrance bounced off the shiny paintwork of the Bentleys and Ferraris and Lamborghinis that were lined up outside like the forecourt of Alexander's fantasy garage.

As she picked her way across the wet cobbles, holding her skirt up so it didn't drag on the ground, she could see through the open doors to rows of marble columns, glowing like gold in the lamplight inside, and hear music—the sexy, high-tempo whine of electric violins.

Oh, God. And now she had to go in there...

It would almost be funny if it weren't so awful. This wasn't her world, and she didn't even want it to be. Much as she grumbled about Hartley Bridge, and the fact that its one shop closed for an hour at lunchtime and sold malt vinegar rather than balsamic, it was where she belonged.

Where she felt safe.

The shivering had turned into a violent trembling that was nothing to do with the cold. High above Monte Carlo, beyond the lights and the noise, the hills were barely distinguishable from the black sky. Somewhere up there was the big empty villa where, on a warm, pine-scented evening in May, her whole life had changed in ways she could never have imagined.

Resolutely she raised her chin. Dominic was right. It was time to take control of things. Things had a habit of happening to her—things out of her control— that served to remind her time and time again of how precarious life was, how fragile and fallible. It was high time she took matters into her own hands for once and faced up to her fears.

Clutching her evening bag in front of her like a shield, she went up the steps and into the gilded and opulent interior.

'So, what do you think? Do you like it?'

Handing him a glass of champagne, Suki came to stand beside Cristiano at the gallery rail. Above the frantic swell of electric violins he could hear the note of triumph in her voice as she looked down on the scene below.

Like it?

A pulse beat in Cristiano's temple, out of time with the music. He felt sweat break out on his forehead.

The party was well underway, and the ornate and imposing salon was filling up with guests—some of whom Cristiano knew well from the racing circuit, and others whose faces he knew only from glossy magazines. At the foot of the wide staircase that swept down from the gallery a raised platform had been erected, on which four ravishing beauties with Perspex electric violins prowled and writhed around two cars.

The Campano car that the team would be running during the forthcoming Grand Prix was being unveiled to the public for the first time tonight. A study of design and engineering perfection, its paintwork glittered in the light of the chandeliers like polished emeralds, and its sleek lines were reminiscent of some crouching, predatory beast.

But it was the other one that people had gathered to look at. The obscene lump of distorted metal that had once been a car and had nearly been his coffin.

'Whether *I* like it is irrelevant,' Cristiano said tonelessly, dragging his gaze away from it. 'Everyone else seems to be fascinated.'

With a hiss of scarlet satin Suki turned, looking at him from under lashes that were too thick and black to be real. 'They're glad that you're back, that's all,' she said throatily, reaching up to straighten his collar unnecessarily. 'You're a hero. Everyone remembers the accident, but seeing the car like that will bring it home to people how amazing you are to have come back from it.'

Her musky perfume caught in the back of his throat, combining with the despair that lodged there, choking him. Everyone remembered the accident *except him*. And if Dr Fournier was right that might mean that, no matter how strong he was, it would never come back.

He knocked back a slug of champagne. It had cost Silvio a fortune, but to him it tasted like battery acid.

'I'm not back yet.'

'But you will be,' Suki purred, trailing a scarlet-tipped finger down the silk lapel of his dinner jacket. 'You were three times World Champion. You just need to get a couple of races—a couple of wins—under your belt. I know it must be hard—'

With a muted sound of disgust Cristiano broke away from her, thrusting both hands through his hair. Apart from Francine Fournier, Suki was the only person who knew about his memory loss, but even she had no idea about the flashbacks and the panic attacks and the palpitations that plagued him when he was driving.

'You don't know the half of it,' he said bitterly.

Below them Silvio was moving swiftly from group to group, beaming as he shook hands with the men and kissed the women, most of whom towered above him in high heels. In a moment he would make a speech, and then after that the guests would disperse into the adjoining salons and take their places at the gaming tables to play poker and roulette. Suki's theme for the evening had been decided apparently without irony, and the guests were looking forward to celebrating Cristiano's return by gambling with Campano money.

For him, the stakes were much higher.

'I'm here for you—you know that,' Suki said in a low voice. 'If there's anything—'

'The twenty-four hours before the crash,' he interrupted through tightly gritted teeth. 'Tell me again. What happened?'

She stiffened slightly, and suddenly her perfectly made-up face was as hard and expressionless as a Venetian mask. 'I've told you,' she said carefully. 'There's nothing more.'

Cristiano's gaze was inexorably pulled back to the shredded metal and blackened paintwork of the ruined car.

'Again,' he said with lethal softness.

He heard her give the merest hint of an impatient sigh. 'You qualified in pole position. Some girl had come over from Clearspring Water to interview you and I took her to the press suite to wait for you while you went back to have a shower and rest.' Her tone was nonchalant, almost as if the events of that lost evening were completely inconsequential. 'One of Silvio's friends was having a party on a yacht, so most of us had left the Campano building by six. I'm guessing that you must have finished your interview with the Clearspring girl by seven and gone home soon afterwards.'

'What about the next morning?'

Suki picked an imaginary bit of lint from the front of her very tight red satin dress. 'Normal race day routine. You arrived at the track—'

'According to the newspapers I missed the drivers' parade.'

'Maybe you were a bit late.' Suki shrugged. 'Four years is a long time. I can't remember exactly what happened that day—none of it seemed to matter compared to what came afterwards.'

The throbbing in his head intensified. The music was building to a crescendo, the violinists thrusting their hips and their bows more and more feverishly as the guests kept coming. Cristiano's gaze flickered restlessly over all of them, as if he was looking for someone in particular.

'Was I alone?'

'When you arrived?' she said casually. 'Of course. Why wouldn't you have been?'

He gave an icy smile. 'Because the night before a race I usually wasn't.'

It seemed like another lifetime. When he had driven fast and won races and seduced women all with the same effortless arrogance.

'Like I said, I was at the party. I didn't see you leave.'

'This girl from Clearspring…'

His voice trailed off and his hand tightened on the

railing as his restless gaze snagged on something below. Someone. He snapped it back, raking his eyes over the crowd again, trying to locate whatever it was that had caused that sensation like a flashbulb going off inside his head.

Suki gave a dismissive laugh. 'Oh, please. She wasn't your type *at all*,' she said with an edge of scorn. 'She turned up wearing some kind of librarian-style grey suit   can you imagine? At Monaco? In May? I'm talking seriously plain and boring—the kind of girl who thinks the best fun you can have in bed is *reading a book...*'

Cristiano had stopped listening.

He was watching the girl in a dress of clinging blue satin who had just walked through the door and was drifting, like the rest of the guests, towards the stage. The thing was, he wasn't sure *why* he was watching her.

Another flashbulb exploded inside his head.

In a roomful of some of the most beautiful women in the world she should have been invisible, but suddenly it was impossible to look at anyone else. She was slight, slender, though the cut of the dress accentuated breasts that looked surprisingly full and lush, and her dark blonde hair was loose and unadorned, curling up slightly at the ends where it skimmed her bare shoulders. There was something very separate about the upright way she held herself, as if she were battling the temptation to turn and run. Her eyes were downcast, her face pale and completely expressionless.

'Who's that?'

His voice sounded as if he'd swallowed a razor-blade. Suki glanced at him in surprise, following his gaze. 'I take it you don't mean the woman in the red Dolce & Gabbana? Because if you don't know who *she* is then—'

'Blue dress.'

'Oh.' Suki made the single syllable bristle with disdain. 'I have no idea—which means she's probably nobody. The girlfriend of one of the minor mechanics or geeky technicians. She looks vaguely familiar, but I can't think where I've seen her before.'

Cristiano didn't answer. The girl was directly below them now, so that he could see the satin sheen of her bare back and the raised bumps of her spine.

This time his head felt as if it had been split in two by forked lightning. It was as if the violinists were dragging their bows backwards and forwards over his taut nerves as their music swooped and screamed towards its pulsing climax. He was distantly aware of pain shooting up the tendons in his forearms, and realised he was gripping the railing so hard that his fingers were numb, as if he was trying to stop himself vaulting over it to get to the girl in the blue dress.

She had come to a standstill a little distance away from the platform where the violinists still tossed their hair and swayed between the two cars. Her back was towards him and Cristiano felt his body tightening, hardening, as his eyes travelled down its bare length. Her skin was the colour of old ivory.

And then suddenly she turned, ducking her head and slipping through the crowd that had gathered behind her. Everyone was too preoccupied with watching the violinists and looking at the wrecked car to take any notice of her as she passed.

Except him.

Her hair fell forward over her face, but just as she passed beneath the gallery where he stood she pushed it back, and he saw that the expression on her face was one of naked anguish.

He didn't think. He didn't hesitate. Thrusting the barely touched glass of champagne back at Suki, he was moving towards the staircase before she could open her mouth.

'Cristiano!' Her voice was high with surprise and indignation. 'Cristiano—where are—?'

But he had already gone.

CHAPTER THREE

THE car was like some kind of gruesome exhibit from her darkest nightmare. Coming across it like that—incongruously displayed in the opulence of the Casino's grand salon like some kind of obscene trophy—made Kate feel faint with horror.

She had to get away. People were pressing around her, trying to get closer to look at the lump of twisted metal, their avid faces blurring into one as Kate struggled to push past. The music was loud enough to make the hot air pulse, and the room seemed to tilt and spin so that she couldn't remember which door she'd come through.

Looking around wildly, she stifled a whimper of panic. Whichever way she turned she seemed to be hemmed in by people—swigging champagne, tossing manes of glossy hair, throwing back their heads and laughing—until she felt as if she was in some grotesque circus. Then miraculously, ahead of her, she saw the tall double doors that led to the lobby. Ducking her head, she gathered up the slippery fall of her skirt and broke into a half-run.

The lobby was empty now, and the cool air from outside fanned across her burning cheeks. The heels of her torturous shoes rang on the marble floor as she headed for the exit, hoping that Lisa or Ian hadn't seen her and might follow and try to persuade her to come back again.

'Wait.'

The word was low and fierce. Oh, God, she was even hearing voices now. Echoes from the past. Just as she did so often in her dreams. Any moment now she'd wake up and find herself staring at the ceiling of her cramped bedroom back in Hartley Bridge. Please God—please let her wake up before the part where she had to watch the car he was driving hit the barrier. Turn over. Burst into flames…

'*Wait!*'

In dreams things happen in slow motion, and that was how it was then. Strong fingers closed around her wrist and she was being pulled back, a powerful wave of shock jolting through her body and her making her head whip round.

Her breath stopped.

He was inches away from her, his face darker, harder, leaner and even more terrifyingly perfect than she remembered. But it was his eyes that made her poor battered heart turn over as they burned into hers with laser-like intensity.

Her lips parted to speak but no sound came out.

And then…

And then his mouth was on hers, his fingers biting

into her shoulders as he gripped her, and kissed her, and she kissed him back with all the pain and loneliness and desperate longing of the last four years. Showers of incredulous joy burst inside her head and spread through her whole body. She felt weak with relief, with joy, as their mouths devoured each other, brutal and ruthless, their tongues probing and fighting, their teeth clashing.

Distantly she was aware of the music coming to a thundering climax, and the eruption of applause—which suddenly got louder as the door behind them opened.

'Cristiano?'

The voice was sharp and impatient, and Cristiano was lifting his head, pulling away from her, and the real world was rushing back in, in a blur of bright light and noise. He let go of her shoulders abruptly.

Kate staggered backwards, her hands flying to her mouth, which pulsed and throbbed, covering the incredulous smile that she couldn't suppress. A beautiful and exotic-looking girl she remembered from Monaco as Cristiano's PA, and whom she had seen coming and going from the hospital, was standing in the doorway. Her slanting, cat-like eyes flickered over Kate before going back to Cristiano.

'Silvio is about to make his speech.'

'*Va bene,*' he said tersely. 'I'll be there in a minute.'

The girl stared at him for a second, as if she wanted to say more, but then she turned and disappeared with a disdainful flick of her black shiny hair. The noise from the crowded room was shut off suddenly as the door closed behind her.

Kate was trembling violently with shock in the aftermath of that kiss, and with a sort of wild, excited anticipation, unable to take in the fact that the moment she'd waited for all these years was finally here.

He was here.

Her gaze travelled wonderingly over him, as if trying to make her dazzled mind believe what she was seeing. She had only ever seen him in racing overalls or jeans and a T-shirt before, but the black, perfectly tailored dinner jacket added a whole new dimension of sexiness to his racing driver's physique, making his shoulders look wider and stronger, his hips narrower. Or maybe they were narrower, she thought with a wrench of desire and compassion. He had lost weight since the accident. The realisation made her want to wrap her arms around him and...

Slowly he turned back to face her. There was a curious stillness about him. In the golden light of the chandeliers his face looked unusually pale.

'*Mi dispiace.* I shouldn't have done that.'

His voice was toneless. Kate felt a pinprick of icy fear at the base of her spine. She shook her head, twisting her hands together to stop herself from reaching out to him.

'It's OK.'

He smiled—a chilling echo of the lazy, sexy, delicious smile she remembered so well.

'Not really. I'm afraid I mistook you for someone else. I apologise…'

The fear blossomed and spread through her, as if it was being injected into her veins. She felt her own smile freeze on her face—a rictus grin of horror. Her whole body suddenly seemed to be made of stone, and it was all she could do to turn her face away so he wouldn't see the desolation and utter humiliation there.

'Kate. It's Kate.'

Her voice was a cracked whisper. She had to leave. Now. Before everything she had ever imagined in her worst-case scenario paled into insignificance.

He nodded curtly, taking a step backwards in the direction of the doors, giving her the benefit of his heartbreaking, ironic half-smile. 'Kate. Forgive me for my…impulsiveness. It was a pleasure to meet you.'

It felt as if she'd been punched hard in the stomach. She wanted to double up and gasp for air. It had been a mistake. She'd thought he'd recognised her. Remembered her. But it had been…a *mistake*.

He turned, his shoulders very rigid as he walked away. In a second he would open the door and go back into the crowded room and she would be alone. The moment would have passed.

'We—we've…met before, actually. I'm from Clearspring Water. I interviewed you…once.'

Oh, God. She sounded desperate. Unbalanced. Like some disturbed, obsessed fan. She wouldn't blame him if he alerted Security now. So to save herself the humiliation of being escorted off the premises, she gathered up her skirt and backed off a couple of steps.

He stopped.

For a moment he was absolutely still, as if turned to stone. Kate had to remind herself to keep breathing. Slowly, stiffly, he turned back to face her.

'Kate Edwards.' His voice was soft, his tone completely neutral, but his face looked as if it had been carved from ice. 'You interviewed me the night before the Monaco Grand Prix four years ago.'

'Yes.'

So he knew. He knew who she was and yet he stood there, looking at her across the cavernous space with eyes that glittered with some emotion she couldn't read, but which certainly wasn't love. Or happiness, or excitement, or relief—or any of the other things *she* had felt when she saw him again. Her heart was beating very hard, very fast, shaking her whole body and pounding in her head as she began to back towards the door.

'I'm glad you're well again. I'm glad you're back— i-if that's what you want…' Her skirt twisted around her legs, slowing her down. She managed a smile, though it felt as if her face might crack. 'It was nice to see you again.'

She was almost at the door. She could feel the cold

night air at her back, and she turned round and covered the remaining few feet as quickly as she could in her agonising high heels. She didn't slow down until she had reached the door of the Hotel de Paris opposite.

It was only then that she remembered the letter in her evening bag.

Silvio's speech was mercifully short. As the crowd clapped and cheered, Cristiano made his way round the back of the platform to where Suki stood.

'I slept with her, didn't I?'

'Who?'

Suki looked up at him with deliberately blank eyes. Cristiano had to grit his teeth, steadying himself against the feeling of panic that was closing in on him. The whole evening had taken on a kind of nightmarish quality, so that he wasn't sure what was real any more.

'Kate Edwards,' he rasped. 'From Clearspring Water. I slept with her the night before the crash. Why didn't you tell me?'

Suki's blank gaze slid away again and she shrugged. 'What does it matter? You slept with everyone.'

Cristiano jerked backwards, raising his hand so that for a moment Suki thought he was going to hit her. He thrust it into his hair and swore, and then swung round and began to push his way through the crowd.

Except me, she wanted to scream after him,

watching his massive shoulders as he walked away, and the way people moved aside to let him through. *Everyone except me.*

Adrenaline burned through Cristiano's veins as he ran down the Casino steps. The cool air, with its whisper of pine and the sea, felt good tasted better than the champagne he'd been avoiding all evening and out in the street-lit darkness the pounding inside his head was less intense. He knew that Silvio would be looking for him now, wanting him to stand in front of the two cars on the platform while the flashbulbs of hundreds of press photographers exploded all around, but he didn't care.

He didn't care about anything except finding Kate Edwards.

She had gone into the Hotel a Paris when she'd run out of here. Standing in the middle of the marble floor, still reeling from the realisation of who she was, he had watched her crossing the square, dodging in front of a car in her haste to get away.

He nodded curtly at the doorman, who leapt forward to open the door for him as Suki's words came back to him. *She wasn't your type at all...seriously plain and boring...*

She was right about the first bit at least Kate Edwards *was* different entirely from the women he usually bedded, and yet there was something about her that tugged like a fish hook in his brain and left him in no doubt that he'd slept with her that night.

And that the experience had been worth remembering.

Worth repeating—especially if it helped him to remember.

The receptionist glanced up from her computer screen as he approached the desk and, seeing who he was, started visibly.

'Can you tell me which room Kate Edwards is in?'

Her pink-painted mouth had fallen open, and she was looking at him in undisguised awe, so it was a second before she answered. '*Pardon*, Signor Maresca…b-but really I shouldn't…'

'I hope Miss Edwards would disagree with that.' He dropped his voice and, looking her straight in the eye, smiled. 'Please?'

Colour flooded into her cheeks as she tapped the keyboard, and Cristiano felt a grim moment of satisfaction. It had been a long time since he'd actively flirted with anyone, but that at least was something he could still do. He just hoped that Kate Edwards would fall for it as easily.

Because she was his best hope of recovering those lost hours. He'd slept with her then—would sleeping with her again bring them back?

So that was it.

After four years of waiting, hoping, dreaming and wishing, it was finally over.

With a shaking hand Kate swept up all the brand-new expensive cosmetics so carefully picked out by Lizzie and shoved them back into her make-up bag. Most of them hadn't even been opened. What a waste of money, she thought, stifling a sob.

But what was money compared to four years of her life?

She pulled her cheap suitcase down from the rack by the door and threw it onto the bed. She didn't intend to waste a second longer on a man who couldn't even remember sleeping with her. A shallow, cold-hearted playboy, with eyes like black ice and a heart of stone.

Straightening up for a moment, she clenched her fists and took in a deep, shuddering breath. Her eyes and her throat burned with the tears that she couldn't shed yet. Not while humiliation and fury and bitterness were still so raw.

And the desire.

Her stomach still fluttered with it, and her legs felt weak and shaky. Passing the long mirror on her way to the wardrobe, she caught sight of her reflection and saw that her eyes were huge and dark-centred, her make-up smudged, her lips red and swollen.

She stopped, one trembling hand flying to her mouth, her rapid heartbeat seeming to echo in the muffled silence of the opulent room as her mind replayed the kiss.

How could she have been so *stupid*?

Not just tonight, she thought bitterly, kissing him like that, but for the last four miserable years. All those nights of waiting, looking out into the darkness and wishing for him. The loneliness of antenatal appointments, when all the other expectant mothers had had their husbands with them and she'd been alone. Visiting times in hospital, when she'd watched proud fathers take their newborns in big, awkward hands and gaze down at them adoringly—all those times when she'd silently wished for Cristiano, silently held onto her memory of his kiss, his touch, the way he'd looked into her eyes that night and the sound of his voice in her head.

This isn't over... Last night was just the beginning. Wait for me.

Well, she *had* waited. And she'd hoped and believed that it was the accident that had kept him away. That somehow he'd been trying to reach her, thinking of her the way that she'd been thinking of him, but that something or someone had stopped him making contact.

How unutterably, embarrassingly stupid that seemed now. She had spent four years pining for a man who didn't exist.

Well, at least tonight hadn't been a *complete* waste of time and expensive make-up. At least she had finally learned that Cristiano Maresca was not the kind of man she wanted as a father for her son. She picked up her velvet evening bag from where she had thrown it on the bed and shoved it into the bottom of her open suitcase, suppressing a shiver of relief that she hadn't handed over the letter. Alexander was better off without him in his life, and Cristiano…

A fat tear wobbled for a second on her eyelashes and then fell, glittering, and sank into the thick blue carpet as she pictured her son. Cristiano didn't deserve to know Alexander, she thought fiercely. Children weren't possessions to be passed between rightful owners. It took more than one night of great sex to make a parent, more than genes and chromosomes. It took love. Selflessness. Dedication. Patience. *Being there*.

And Cristiano Maresca didn't qualify on any of those counts.

Gathering herself, she yanked open the wardrobe door. Suddenly aware that she was shaking violently, she pulled on the polo-necked jumper that her mother had given her for Christmas over the blue dress and began bundling up the rest of her things and shoving them back into the case from which she'd so recently unfolded them.

A knock at the door made her jump. It must be the concierge, with information about changing her flight home, she thought with a surge of relief, throwing an armful of underwear on the top of the bag and rushing to answer it. Please God, let him have found her a seat on a plane tonight—

She had only opened the door a crack when she realised her mistake.

It wasn't the concierge who stood there.

It was Cristiano Maresca.

A jolt of electricity shot through her, and acting on pure adrenaline-fuelled instinct she went to slam the door in his face. But he was too quick for her. Too quick and too strong. Before she knew it she was stumbling backwards as he thrust his body into the gap between the door and the wall.

'Wh-what are you doing here?'

Kate's chest was rising and falling rapidly, her breath coming in uneven gasps, but he was perfectly unruffled. His face was completely expressionless, his eyes dark and opaque.

'I want to talk to you,' he said softly.

Kate couldn't stop the bitter laugh from escaping her. 'Really? That wasn't what it looked like back there.'

Her voice was breathless and shaky. He made no move towards her, but her heart was hammering viciously against her ribs, and beneath the jumper she was suddenly boiling hot.

'We were interrupted.' Leaning back against the wall with deceptive nonchalance, he was still looking at her steadily. 'I hoped you'd wait.'

'I did.' Suddenly the narrow space by the door seemed horribly claustrophobic. Whirling round, Kate walked quickly back into the room, desperate to put some space between them. 'Last time. I waited last time—remember?'

'What?'

Something in his tone made her turn back to look at him. He had levered himself away from the wall and was advancing across the room towards her, his eyes burning with an intensity that was almost frightening.

'Forget it,' she muttered, going into the bathroom to collect the things she'd left in there. 'It doesn't matter.'

She threw her toothbrush into her washbag and, going out again, collided with him in the doorway.

Before she could back away, he caught hold of her shoulders and looked down at her with a twisted, ironic smile that skewered her heart. 'Actually, it does.' Noticing the washbag, he frowned. 'What are you doing?'

'Packing. I'm going home.'

His grip on her shoulders didn't loosen, but his gaze shifted from hers, sliding downwards. 'That's a shame,' he said gravely. 'I would have liked to get to know you better.' He lifted a hand, brushing a strand of hair back from her cheek. In the soft light his face wore an abstracted expression, and was almost impossibly perfect. 'Could I persuade you to stay?'

Agonising desire zigzagged through her like lightning, rooting her to the spot for a second as every nerve in her body sang beneath his touch and her senses reeled at his nearness. For all this time she had carried the scent of his skin in her memory, and now it was in her head, and the eyes she had looked into so often in her dreams were staring straight back into hers...

But their expression was different now. Gone was

the emotion that had reached inside her and tugged her heart from her chest, and in its place was something darker. Harder. Colder.

'No.'

Wrenching herself away, she took a couple of steps backwards, gathering up folds of satin, twisting them in her damp fists as she walked around to the other side of the pristine hotel bed. 'I don't want to be another notch on your bedpost, another anonymous name on your list of one-night stands.' Grabbing her case, she viciously shoved the washbag into it and gave a shaky, slightly hysterical laugh. 'I suppose that if you take into account that night four years ago that would technically make it a *two*-night stand, but it would also make me doubly stupid to fall for the same routine tw—'

The knock at the door made her jump and stopped her mid-sentence. Rushing to open it, she was dimly aware that she was still wearing the blue satin dress and had just put all the rest of her clothes in the suitcase. What was it about Cristiano Maresca that made it impossible to think straight?

'Good evening, *mademoiselle*.'

It was the concierge—a short, sleek man, with a neat moustache like Hercule Poirot. A strange mixture of relief and panic churned inside her at the thought of leaving here now. Walking away down the wide, thick-carpeted corridor. Walking away from Cristiano for good.

'You asked to be booked on a flight back to Leeds,

England, as soon as possible?' the concierge asked politely.

'Yes. I'll just get my—'

'*Pardonez-moi, mademoiselle*, but I'm afraid I have bad news. Due to thick fog over Leeds tonight many flights have been cancelled, and the remaining ones are being diverted to Heathrow. I'm afraid there are no seats available on any UK flight with any airline at the moment.'

Kate felt the air whoosh from her lungs and the ground tilt a little beneath her feet as she took in this information. It felt like absorbing a physical blow.

'But that can't be right, surely? There must be something...'

'I'm afraid not, *mademoiselle*,' the concierge murmured gravely. 'I have checked with all the airlines. Of course,' he added doubtfully, glancing at her very obviously un-designer jumper, 'if it is urgent I could possibly look into a private charter...?'

Kate shook her head, swallowing back the hysterical bubble of laughter that rose inside her. Dominic was notoriously relaxed when it came to expenses, but she suspected that even he might balk at private jet hire. And, since most weeks she struggled to afford petrol for her ancient car, it certainly wasn't going to come out of her own pocket.

'Very well, *mademoiselle*.' The concierge gave a little bow. 'I am sorry not to have been able to help. If there's anything more I can do for you, please don't hesitate to call down to Reception.'

'Thank you,' Kate murmured faintly, shutting the door behind his departing back and leaning against it for a moment while she struggled to control her desolation.

She wanted so much to go home—back to Alexander. Dominic had given them all a week off to enjoy the considerable luxury of the hotel and explore the city, so their scheduled flight home wasn't until Friday. She hadn't argued because, she now realised, deep down she'd secretly hoped that she'd be with Cristiano.

Stupid, stupid, stupid.

She turned round abruptly, gritting her teeth as a crashing wave of homesickness and despair washed over her, not knowing what to do now. Cristiano was at the window. He had pulled the curtain back and was standing by the doors to the balcony, the lurid lights from the square outside casting hollows beneath his cheekbones and making his olive skin look strangely bleached of colour.

'So, it looks like you're not going home after all,' he said, without turning round to look at her.

'You don't have to sound so pleased.' She hated the bitterness and misery in her tone, but was suddenly too tired to hide them any more. Too tired to pretend.

He dropped the curtain, so his face was suddenly plunged into shadow again.

'I don't want you to run away until we've had a chance to talk.'

'What about?'

Oh, God. For the first time it occurred to her that he might somehow have already found out about Alexander. Nausea rolled through her. She wanted to sink down onto the bed, but knew she'd feel at a disadvantage with him towering over her, so settled instead for perching on the edge of the dressing table. Her heart was battering against her ribs as he came towards her, and she searched his face for clues.

There were none. Apart from a muscle flickering in his lean, tanned cheek it was very still and completely blank.

'The night we spent together.'

She gave an anxious laugh. 'I don't know why. It clearly didn't make it onto your list of top ten one-night stands, so unless you need the details to put in some kind of no-holds barred, X-rated autobiography there's really not much point in going over it.' Nerves were making her talk too much, too fast, and tears stung at the back of her eyes. 'It's funny,' she went on. 'Although on some level I understand that when you sleep with a man who is known throughout the world as a heart-breaking, womanising playboy you can't exactly expect flowers and a card on your anniversary, it would at least be nice to think that he'd recognise you again. Especially after—'

She stopped, suddenly breathless. An image, suppressed for the last four years, rose to the surface of her mind. The sun rising over the sea, bathing their naked bodies in rosy pink light, painting streaks of gold into his hair while, bleak-faced and rigid, he told her about his past.

'After what?'

The man in front of her looked the same—agonisingly, mockingly the same—and yet so different. Tears welled in her eyes and she got sharply to her feet.

'Forget it.' Impatiently she dashed the tears away as she made to move past him, and gave a broken laugh. 'Oh, but of course you already have—haven't you?'

He gave a low, savage curse. Catching hold of her arm, he pulled her back so that she hit the hard wall of his chest.

'Yes,' he rasped, his face ashen, his eyes like glittering pools of tar. 'Yes, I bloody well have. I've forgotten *everything* from the time I got into that car to qualify for the race to the moment I hit the barrier. It's lost. Twenty-four hours of nothingness. So that's why we need to talk. I want to know what happened.'

For a long, shivering moment it felt as if time had stopped as their gazes locked. But then her hoarse whisper broke the silence. Broke the spell.

'Oh, God, Cristiano. I—I'm sorry.'

Letting go of her abruptly, Cristiano spun round and walked back to the window, raising a hand to his pounding forehead. Why the hell had he just said that? He had come up here to get out of her whatever he could, using whatever means it took—he had intended to *seduce* her, not confide in her, *per l'amore di Dio*. He didn't want anyone to know about this. Never mind some girl he didn't know, didn't trust not to go to the papers.

'I had no idea.'

'No. Well, it's not exactly something I want to broadcast,' he said icily.

'But why?' There was a curious tension in her voice, and the light from the lamp beside her turned her skin to gold satin and reflected in her eyes, making it look as if there was a flame leaping in their depths. 'I mean, you had a terrible accident, and people would—'

'Love to know that I'm not over it?' He cut her off sharply, as if that would also help him cut off the urge to cross the room and take her face in his hands and kiss that soft mouth again. 'That I have this…this *gap*? Can you imagine what would happen if it got out that I have no memory of that evening? How many women would come forward and claim I was with them? That I slept with them, assaulted them, fathered their children? The tabloid newspapers would have enough salacious front pages for the next three years, and there would be nothing I could do— *nothing*—because *I can't remember.*'

'Oh.' It was more like a defeated exhalation than a properly enunciated word. Tugging her jumper down over her hands, as if she was cold, she shook her head slightly, so that her soft hair shimmered in the light of the lamp. 'I didn't think of it like that. Why would anyone do that? Make things up?'

He gave a harsh laugh. 'How about for five minutes of fame and a few hundred grand? Even if a story could be disproved, with a DNA test or an alibi, by that time the damage would already have been done.'

She stood up, wrapping her arms around herself for a moment and looking around as if she was disorientated. 'Well, you don't need to worry about that any more. You were with me.' She looked at him then, straight in the eye, and gave a painful smile that seemed to reach down inside him and twist at his heart. '*I* know what happened, and I promise you I'm not going to spread it all over the front pages. You can relax. Get back to your party and your adoring fans and stop worrying about it.'

Her voice was soft, resigned. Cristiano tried to focus on what she was saying—to make sense of it—but the ache in his head had intensified so that it felt as if someone was hitting the inside of his skull with a sledgehammer.

'I have no intention of going back,' he said tersely, remembering how he had planned to spend the rest of the night. In bed with her. Seducing her into telling him everything he so badly wanted to know. But he had underestimated her, he realised now. He had assumed she would fall into bed with him at the merest hint of an opportunity, like any one of the scores of women across the square who were no doubt searching the Casino for him right now. The fact that she hadn't was intriguing, as well as surprisingly painfully frustrating.

He thrust his hands in his pockets, gritting his teeth against the throbbing in his head—and in other, more basic parts of his anatomy. 'I'm going away for a while.'

She had moved across to the bed again and was leaning forward, unzipping the case she'd just finished packing. Her hand stilled. 'Oh? Where to?'

'A chalet in the Alps. It belongs to a friend.'

His voice was rough in the quiet room. From a long way off he could just about hear the sounds of the party in the Casino—the pulse of the music and the muffled sound of a lot of voices raised to speak over it. Suddenly he was profoundly glad to have escaped.

To be here.

Slowly she lifted her head and looked up. Her eyes were wide, the blue almost swallowed up by the darkness at their centre.

'You're going tonight?'

He nodded, not letting his gaze move from hers. Not able to. 'I'm going now.'

Her tongue darted out and moistened her lips. 'Alone?'

It was barely more than a whisper, and it felt like a caress. Cristiano felt desire slam into him with all the force of a head-on collision. The air between them throbbed with sudden possibility.

'I hope not,' he said softly.

CHAPTER FOUR

IT WAS a starless night.

Sitting in the low passenger seat of Cristiano's expensive sports car, Kate bit her lip and stared out into the darkness, trying to stop the convulsive tremors that gripped her

The car's headlamps lit the empty road ahead, but beyond them there was nothing but velvet blackness. She had no idea where they were, or exactly where they were going. There was no north star to use as a compass, no moon to light the way.

It seemed crushingly symbolic.

The surge of hope she had felt when he'd told her about his memory loss had completely ebbed away now, leaving a hollow despair in its place. At first she had been overwhelmed with relief that there was a reason why he had forgotten her, that it wasn't that she just hadn't been significant enough for him to remember. It had all seemed so wonderfully simple—as if someone had handed her the missing part of the jigsaw, the vital clue that made sense of the last four years. She had barely hesitated for a heartbeat when he asked her to go with him.

But it wasn't simple at all.

She was nothing more than a stranger to him now. The crash hadn't just stolen a few hours from his memory, it had also robbed him of the ability to trust. If she told him what they'd shared that night he'd think she was one of those grasping fantasists he'd described in the hotel room, not only demanding money and fame but something more sinister and exploitative.

Demanding his heart.

She clasped her hands together in her lap to stop her fingers nervously pleating the blue satin dress she hadn't even thought to change out of. At that moment he looked across at her. The greenish light of the high-tech instrument panel gave his perfect face a chilling remoteness which seemed to reinforce her worst fears.

'OK?'

She nodded quickly, struggling to find something harmless to say. 'It's a very impressive car.'

Alex would adore it, she thought with a stab of anguish.

'It's the latest Campano sports model,' Cristiano said tonelessly, slowing down as a lorry appeared in front of them. 'I'm testing it for Silvio so I can casually mention it in every interview I do at the start of the racing season.'

He was *meant* to be testing it anyway, he thought

wearily, although the way he was driving it tonight was hardly doing justice to its almost mythical capabilities. For some reason having her in the passenger seat was making him stick to speed limits and hold back from overtaking cars he would otherwise have left standing.

'How far is it to where we're going?' Kate asked, looking out to where the first snowy peaks of the Alps loomed palely in the distance.

There was something about her tone that made him think she was regretting coming almost as much as he was beginning to regret asking her. He should have talked to her back in the hotel. Made her go over the events of that night and then left for the chalet in the morning. Alone.

'Probably about another three hours. It's right up in the mountains, so the roads aren't great. Do you ski?'

She bent her head so that her face was screened from his view by the soft curtain of her hair. 'I'm afraid not.'

She wasn't your type at all.

Suki's words came back to mock him, and he felt his lips quirk into an ironic smile of tacit acknowledgement. All his girlfriends skied and snowboarded and scuba-dived. As well as having supermodel looks, those were pretty much the qualifications for the job.

'I'll just have to teach you, then.'

'In this?' She gave a nervous laugh, her fingers

plucking at the slippery fabric of her evening dress. Long fingers, he noticed. Long and delicate. 'I've hardly got the right clothes for skiing.'

He looked back at the road again, frowning. 'I'm sure Francine has ski stuff there you can borrow.'

'Francine?' There was a tiny note of alarm in her voice.

'My neurologist. It's her house.'

And her idea, he thought grimly. Right now it didn't feel like one of her better ones. Already the thought of being away from the track and the team was making him feel on edge, and that feeling was only exacerbated by the idea of being *with* Kate Edwards. It would have been one thing seducing her in the hotel, spending the night with her to see if it brought back any memories of the last time, but spending a couple of days alone with her was quite another. The whole point of the exercise had been to relax, *per l'amore di Dio*.

'Anyway, I'd be rubbish at skiing,' she was saying now, in her soft, low voice. 'And terrified. I'm the girl who had to be rescued from halfway up an indoor climbing wall on a Clearspring team-building exercise. I'm the least white-knuckle person on the planet. That night when we—'

She broke off. Cristiano glanced across at her sharply.

'Go on. Tell me.'

'That night in Monaco, you drove me from the track to your house to do the interview.' She darted him a sideways look and smiled shyly. 'I was scared out of my wits by your driving.'

He gave an ironic smile, but in the light of a passing car Kate noticed that he was gripping the steering wheel so tightly that his knuckles showed bone-white through his tanned skin. 'With good reason, as it turned out,' he said cuttingly. 'Given what happened the next day.'

'Don't,' she muttered in anguish, closing her eyes and tensing as he pulled out to overtake the lorry they'd been following for the last few miles. The car surged forward with a powerful, muted roar. When Cristiano spoke again his voice was thoughtful.

'You're not much of a fan of motor racing, are you?'

'No,' she admitted, staring dully out at the dark houses of the small town they were driving through, picturing the children asleep behind the closed shutters. 'But my brother was a huge fan of yours, which meant I was just about clued up enough to do the interview.'

'Was?'

'He'd been killed in a car accident the year before.' She attempted a rueful laugh. 'That's probably why I freaked out about your driving—and the fact that my dad had died the same way when I was younger. Cars have always made me nervous, and Will's death was still a bit raw.'

Letting go of the steering wheel, Cristiano rubbed

a hand over his face. 'Did you tell me about it at the time?'

Kate leaned her head back against the leather upholstery. She felt suddenly very tired. 'Not while we were in the car.' She gave a faint smile. 'I was too scared to open my mouth then. But we talked about it…later.'

God, she remembered it as if it was yesterday. She'd been so disapproving of Cristiano Maresca and what he did for a living, so determined to be cool and professional and not to be swayed by his legendary good-looks and notorious sex appeal. But the moment she'd reluctantly lowered herself into the passenger seat of his terrifying car her pretence at sophisticated detachment had been completely shattered. By the time they'd reached his villa in the hills she'd been a wreck—a fact that had been impossible to disguise. It had also broken down the professional distance between them.

She closed her eyes, shifting restlessly in her seat as jagged arrows of desire pierced her, not wanting to think about what had happened next.

'Do you feel scared now?'

In the velvet darkness behind her closed lids Cristiano's voice was like gravel. But still it made her shiver, because it was the voice that she had heard in her dreams for so long.

Mutely she shook her head.

Not of the car or the road anyway. But the strength

and force of her own longing, held in check for all these years, terrified her.

As they drove further north the clouds parted and the stars came out. It was suddenly much colder. Stopping for petrol and to fit snow chains on the tyres, Cristiano could feel the ice in the air. The mountains lay all around, like giant slumberous beasts.

Walking back to the car, after paying the awe-struck teenage boy in the kiosk for the petrol, he flexed his cramped shoulders, putting off the moment when he'd have to get back into the driving seat. The Campano CX8 might be hailed as one of the fastest and most desirable cars in the world, but it wasn't going to be winning any awards for its spacious interior. Something about the intimacy of the small space; the warmth inside and the cool scent of Kate Edwards' skin, the darkness and cold outside, made him feel restless and edgy.

As he reached the car he saw that she was still asleep, and felt an unfamiliar clenching sensation in his chest. Frustration, probably, he told himself sourly as he opened the door and slid into the driver's seat. If he'd been alone he would have reached the chalet ages ago.

Starting the engine, he thought about what she'd said. She'd been afraid in the car with him before, because of her brother. Did that explain why, from the moment they'd left Monte Carlo, he'd been driving with such uncharacteristic caution? On some level did he *know* about her fear? Somehow, somewhere in his head, did he *remember*?

His mind raced as possibilities rushed through it. And hope. He'd recognised her. Not consciously, but as soon as he'd seen her at the party earlier he'd responded viscerally—physically, dammit—proving that his body remembered her even if his head didn't. That was a good sign, wasn't it? All those memories were there. He just needed to access them, and hopefully spending the next twenty-four hours with her would see to that.

The powerful V8 engine gave a gratifying roar as he pulled away from the garage, the kiosk attendant watching open-mouthed through the window.

There were lots of tunnels on the road up into the mountains, and every one he drove through brought his thoughts back to the one at Monaco, where his car had left the track and hit the barrier. He'd watched the footage countless times, but still he couldn't remember it. Six weeks until the start of the season, he thought bleakly. Abandoning his rigorous training schedule at this stage was a huge gamble—God only knew what Silvio would say when he found out. But ultimately he had no choice. He'd do whatever it took, gamble everything he had, to get his life back.

Because if he lost this, he lost everything. There was nothing else. Never had been. He had been a sixteen-year-old on a fast track to self-destruction when he'd spotted Silvio's car parked outside the theatre in Naples on that hot summer night and hotwired it. If Silvio hadn't given him a chance, hadn't seen some glimmer of potential in him that had singularly eluded both his mother and the nuns at school, Cristiano would almost certainly have been in prison long ago. Or dead.

Racing wasn't just his career, it was his life. It was his means of proving to the world that he wasn't the failure everyone had told him he was as a boy. And winning was his justification for destroying his mother's life. His vindication.

A not-quite-complete moon had broken free from behind the mountaintops and now floated above him, turning the road ahead into a river of silver and making diamonds glitter in the snow at the side of it. Eventually a sign for the exclusive mountain resort where Francine Fournier's chalet was situated loomed out of the darkness. As he turned off the main road onto the narrow mountain pass Kate stirred, arching her back and seeming to fight for a moment against the restriction of the seatbelt. Cristiano kept his eyes resolutely fixed on the narrow road ahead as the Campano's wheels spun on the ice and Kate's head fell sideways onto his shoulder.

He stiffened instantly, gritting his teeth as the pulse in his head was joined by an increase in the persistent throb of desire that he had been trying to ignore for the last four hours. Scowling out into the darkness, he tried to block out the butterfly whisper of her breath against his throat, the scent of her hair, and concentrate instead on finding Francine's house...

* * *

Chalet les Pins.

The headlamps lit up the sign on the gatepost—and the huge snowflakes that were now silently swirling out of the blackness. *Grazie a Dio.* Cristiano felt dizzy with exhaustion as he drove the last two hundred metres down the track towards the house and switched the engine off.

There was a light on over the porch of the chalet. He opened the car door and got out stiffly, taking care not to move suddenly and wake Kate as the icy air rushed at him like an avalanche. Collecting the bags from the Campano's tiny boot, he wearily climbed the steps and unlocked the front door, depositing them just inside and switching on the light before going back to get her.

He opened the passenger door. She had barely stirred for the last couple of hours and was still deeply asleep, so that even the sudden cold didn't wake her. Turned sideways in the seat towards him, she had one hand tucked under her cheek. The car's harsh interior light gave her skin an unearthly pallor and made her long lashes cast spiky shadows over her cheeks.

He couldn't bring himself to wake her. Gathering her into his arms, taking care not to hit her head on the low roof as he eased her out of the car, he felt an odd, light-headed sensation. Her body was pliant and warm against his, and he had to clench his jaw against the lust that stabbed him in the gut as she sighed and shifted in his arms. He kicked the car door shut behind him.

Her eyelids flickered, and he felt her stiffen. He tightened his grip.

'Mmm?'

'It's OK.' His voice, rusty from the long hours of silence, seemed to echo slightly in the cavernous night. 'We're here. Go back to sleep.'

Inside the house it was blissfully warm. The front door opened straight into a large open-plan room that was typically Alpine in style, and as he headed straight for the stairs that rose from one end Cristiano was vaguely aware of a huge sofa in front of the central fireplace, soft rugs in faded shades of crimson and indigo, and the soothing scent of woodsmoke and pine resin. He felt a moment of gratitude to Francine Fournier.

At the top of the stairs he pushed open the nearest door. The room was filled with moonlight from a large window, and it fell across a bed. Gently he placed Kate down on it, feeling her body go momentarily rigid as he let her go.

She breathed in sharply, struggling to sit up. An expression of exquisite desolation flickered across her face.

'Cristiano...'

'I'm here.' He answered automatically, instinctively lowering his voice to a whisper in the velvety silence of the dark house.

Her eyes opened. They were filled with anguish, swimming with tears. For a moment they fixed on his face with a sort of hazy, unfocused pain, and then they closed again, the tears silently spilling over.

'Kate...'

His heart faltered. Without thinking he lowered himself to sit on the bed beside her and pulled her against him, pressing his mouth against her hair and murmuring soothing sounds that were somewhere between English and Italian. Her hair smelled clean and sweet, and her body felt soft and voluptuous in his arms.

Unlike his. His body felt uncomfortably taut and rigid.

He lay very still, his teeth gritted against the huge, powerful waves of lust and want that battered against him, not daring to move, calling up every ounce of the iron self-discipline and will-power that had got him through the last four years. And then, very gently, he felt her pull back from him and raise her head, so that she was looking up into his face.

'You really *are* here...' she breathed.

And then, as if compelled by primitive forces completely outside their control, their mouths met. Kate's limbs were stiff, and chilled from sleeping in the cramped seat, but the touch of Cristiano's lips against hers brought her to life again, until her body was flaming and fluid with want.

She was still in some place halfway between sleeping and waking. Dimly she was aware of warmth, the scent of woodsmoke that filled the house, and moonlight spilling silver through the window onto the blissfully smooth sheets of a bed. But all of that was simply a background to the otherworldly ecstasy of his kiss. The anguish of the familiar dream still lingered, firing her with a fierce, focused passion, and as her fingers slid into his silken hair her senses reeled with the scent of his skin—carried in her head all this time.

She clutched at his back and felt hard muscles moving beneath her palms as he tore his mouth from hers and gazed down at her with eyes that burned through the half-light.

'Kate...?'

It was a thousand questions in a single rasping word. She answered them by slowly reaching up and pulling off the jumper she had put on over her dress earlier that night. Her cheeks were still wet with the tears she had shed when she'd thought this was just another dream, another goodbye.

She'd said goodbye to him so many times in her dreams these last four years and woken alone. But now he was here, and the sheer miracle of that fact made her uncharacteristically bold. She wanted him. She had wanted him for so long that her body cried out with an urgency that wouldn't be hushed until he was inside her.

Her eyes never left his face. It was set like granite—as cool and pale and expressionless as an effigy on a tomb—but she saw the flare of molten desire in his eyes and it made her blood quicken and sing. Reaching up, she began to undo the buttons of his shirt with shaking fingers. Delicious, desperate want was building inside her like a silent scream as, inch by inch, his olive-skinned chest was revealed.

With a muffled curse he brought his hand up, trapping hers.

'Is this what you want?' he growled.

'Yes.' Her voice was a breathless shivering whisper. 'I want *you*.' Freeing her hands from beneath his, she reached up and took his face between them, speaking with ferocious longing into his eyes. 'I want you to *remember*.'

For a second they gazed mutely at each other, and then with a sort of moan of surrender he was pulling her against him as his mouth came down on hers. The quiet room was filled with the sound of their breathing, the rustle of satin, and Kate's whimper of bliss as his hand slid beneath her skirt to meet the bare flesh of her thigh. Arching her back reflexively, she lifted her knees, bringing them up around his waist, opening herself for him.

The bed was soft and wide, and the black and silver world of moonlight and shadow beyond it had ceased to exist. Their fingers tangled together as they both fumbled with the buckle of Cristiano's belt. Kate raised her hips, desperate to be free of the tiny silk knickers Lizzie had insisted on buying, wriggling out of them and spreading herself starfish-like, throbbing with anticipation, on the feather quilt.

Every inch of her skin tingled with the need for

his touch. She wanted him—all of him—on her and in her, with an urgency that struck her dumb.

But he understood. His hands moved up the insides of her thighs. Big hands. Clever, strong, capable hands. Expert hands that left a quivering trail of rapture in their wake. His face was inches from hers. Their mouths opened and clashed again in a searing, devouring kiss before he pulled back again, holding her in his dark, hypnotic gaze as he entered her.

Oh, God, the relief. The screaming, delirious relief and joy and rightness turned her boneless and emptied her head of thought. She grasped a fistful of his silken hair as the rhythm of their movements grew more urgent and the old wooden bed creaked with every hard, hungry thrust.

Bliss opened up in front of her like a chasm. She felt Cristiano falter, heard his indrawn breath as his body tensed, and for a shimmering, breathless moment she teetered on the brink as time stopped and tears rained down her cheeks. And then she was falling, her fingers digging into the hard muscle of his back as she hurtled downwards into ecstasy.

Her high cry of pleasure echoed through the dark house, then faded into silence. Downstairs a clock ticked steadily, and the mountains stood around like watchful sentinels, impassive witnesses to her fragile joy.

CHAPTER FIVE

Dawn came, painting the sky a translucent and delicate shell-pink. Kate watched the last few diamond stars blur and dissolve, and the moon fade until it was little more than a pale fingerprint.

She had slept little and woken when it was still dark, watching as the room that had been no more than a shadowy background to last night's bliss gradually assembled itself into wood-panelled walls, a sloping, heavily beamed roof, solid pieces of furniture. Cristiano's arm was hooked around her waist, his hand resting between her breasts, his body hard and delicious at her back.

She felt warm, sated, oddly at peace. It was as if her brain, shocked by an overload of pleasure last night, had simply shut down, leaving nothing but the physical sensations of the moment. The past seemed as distant and unreal as a bad dream, and the future beyond this room, this wooden house surrounded by pine trees and snow-covered mountains, was impossible to contemplate.

She stretched her legs out, twisting carefully onto

her back so that she could look into Cristiano's sleeping face. He stirred slightly, moving his arm and letting it come to rest again with his palm against her midriff, but his dark lashes barely flickered.

She felt her heart crack open.

Against the white pillow, beside her pale English skin, his was exotically dark, but aside from that, and the shadow of stubble on his jaw, every line of his face reminded her with exquisite poignancy of Alexander. She let her gaze wander over his fine dark brows and perfectly straight nose, downwards to the steep curve of his upper lip, the slight indentation in the lower one, the firm, square chin.

God, he was so beautiful. But, more than that, he was the man who had helped create the little boy she loved so much. The father of her child.

Gently she eased herself out of his arms and slid out of the bed. Taking great care not to wake him, she reached for the shirt he had worn last night and slipped her arms into it, then picked up her velvet evening bag from a red-upholstered armchair and opened it up to get out her phone.

Beside it was the letter. The letter with its bald lines stating the facts of Alexander's existence, the address of the sterile solicitor's office where any further contact should be directed. She felt a small pulse of pain and quickly snapped the clasp shut again. Dropping the bag back onto the chair, she tiptoed out of the room.

None of the curtains had been closed, so the clear

pink light flooded in, making it easy for her to find her way downstairs. It was like a treehouse, Kate thought in wonder as she made her way silently through the smoke-scented living room and into the kitchen. Everything—from the panelled walls and beamed ceilings to the rug-strewn floor and hand-made kitchen cupboards—was made of polished, mellow wood. As she filled the kettle at the huge porcelain sink she felt like Goldilocks, making herself at home in the house of the Three Bears. Champagne bottles clinked in the door of the fridge as she opened it to look for milk, and she saw that the shelves were stocked with eggs, slender packets of smoked salmon, and paper-wrapped parcels of butter and cheese.

Francine Fournier was a life-saver in more ways than one, she thought wryly.

A Scandinavian long-case clock ticked softly at one end of the low room, and, glancing at it, Kate picked up her phone. It was still very early, and an hour earlier in England, but as both Alexander and Ruby were horribly early risers it was highly likely that Lizzie and Dominic would have been up for a while. Waiting for one of them to answer, Kate looked out of the window at the silent mountains, as pink as marsh-mallow in the rising sun, and pictured their familiar big, untidy kitchen. She felt as if she was on another planet, rather than merely in another country.

'Hello?' The voice on the other end of the line sounded distracted.

'Lizzie—it's me.' In the silent house Kate kept her voice low. 'Did I wake you?'

'Kate, honey! Of course you didn't wake me—we're on our second game of Snakes and Ladders here. I just didn't expect *you* to be up this early. You're supposed to be either lazing around in bed and making the most of valuable child-free time to sleep, or having wild sex with the gorgeous Signor Maresca.'

'Well…' Kate found she was smiling as her insides constricted sharply at the memory of last night.

There was an ear-splitting squeal at the other end of the line. 'Kate, you didn't! Oh. My. God. He recognised you?'

Kate felt her smile fade again. 'Not exactly. It's a long story. But I'm with him…'

'He's there now?' Lizzie dropped her voice to a theatrical whisper. 'Have you told him about Alexander?'

'No. And no.' The kettle had finished boiling and, wedging the phone against her ear, Kate spooned coffee into a glass cafetière and poured on water. 'It's not that simple.'

That was an understatement. She didn't know where to begin to explain about Cristiano not being able to remember her, but suddenly she realised that that wasn't actually the most important thing. She frowned. 'He's not how I remembered him, Lizzie. It's not…the same.' She paused, a shiver running through her as she remembered the hardness of his face when he'd looked at her in the Casino, the chips of ice in his eyes. Outside the window the sun had just begun to appear over the top of the mountains, pouring down biblical beams of gold. Kate closed her eyes, feeling its tentative warmth on her cheek.

'Well, that's not surprising.' Lizzie's voice, with its familiar, down-to-earth Yorkshire vowels, was reassuringly brisk. 'Four years is a long time, and a lot has happened to you both. But the main thing is that you're with him, and the old chemistry is obviously still there. You just have to come out with it.'

'It's not the kind of thing you can just casually drop into conversation.'

In her head it had been clear-cut, black and white: either he would reject her completely or—and she had hardly allowed herself to go down this route—they would have the kind of emotional reunion people did in films, just before the credits rolled, accompanied by a lot of swelling music and preferably a sunset. Not for a moment had she considered finding herself in this position. Being with him, back in his bed…but a million miles from the place they had been last time. The place he didn't even know existed now, to which she somehow had to try to find her way back.

'I don't want him to feel like I've trapped him,' she said softly. 'I don't want to force him into anything.'

'You're hardly forcing him—or rushing him, for that matter.'

Kate could vividly imagine Lizzie raising her eyes to heaven as she spoke.

'You've been bringing his son up single-handed for the last three years, and you didn't exactly have a lot of choice about it.'

'I know.' Kate sighed. Lizzie was on her side, she knew that, but she also knew that she would never understand. Strong, forthright Lizzie would never recognise the feeling Kate had now—as if she was cradling a butterfly between her hands, afraid of holding it so tightly she crushed it, afraid of letting it go and watching it fly away. 'It's just I'm scared—'

'Now, look—don't do your usual trick of jumping straight into the worst-case scenario.' Lizzie cut her off, sounding suddenly distracted and impatient. In the background Kate could hear a child crying. A frisson of alarm ran through her.

'Is that Alexander? Is everything all right?'

The line crackled and her own voice echoed back in her ear, sharp with anxiety.

'Everything's fine.' Was it the slight delay on the line, or did Lizzie hesitate before answering? 'Now, go and get straight back into bed with your man, and stop worrying about everything. Have a fabulous time, and we'll speak later, honey—OK?'

'OK. Thanks, Lizzie. Give Alexander a big kiss from me, won't you? And tell him...'

She trailed off, picturing Alexander's sweet face as emotion swelled inside her.

'Sorry, what was that?'

'Just that I love him. And I'll be home soon.'

But as she cut the call she found she didn't want to think about that.

Ten minutes later, very carefully balancing a tray laden with fresh coffee, warm brioche, yellow Normandy butter from the fridge and a jar of honey that had been left on the worktop, Kate gently pushed open the bedroom door.

The sun spilled into the room, warming the bare-boarded floor and turning the tangle of crisp white linen on the bed into a mini-replica of the snowy landscape outside. Cristiano was lying on his front, one bronzed, muscular arm thrown out across the pillows. The duvet lay loosely over his hips, exposing his bare back.

Glancing at him, Kate instantly felt her throat dry, and the china on the tray rattled as a tremor of pure lust went through her. He was a study in masculine perfection—a Leonardo sketch brought to warm, satin-skinned life. The muscles of his massive shoulders were clearly defined, the ridges of his ribs visible beneath the butterscotch-coloured flesh where his body tapered down to his narrow hips.

'*Buongiorno.*'

She jumped, placing the objects on the tray in further jeopardy and letting out a little gasp of shock. She'd been so busy gazing at his delicious body that she hadn't noticed that his dark, hooded eyes were half open and he was watching her.

'Oh…S-sorry,' she stammered as the colour flooded into her cheeks. 'I'm just…I mean, I was trying not to…wake you.'

He sat up in one lithe, rippling movement, like a panther uncurling itself, and pushed his tousled hair back from his forehead.

'I was awake already.' His voice was deep and husky with sleep.

Setting the tray down on the edge of the bed, Kate busied herself moving things around on it to stop herself from staring at him with her mouth open.

'I heard you talking downstairs.'

'I was on the phone.' Oh, God, she hoped he hadn't heard what she was saying. She could feel her blush intensify as she looked up at him through her hair and smiled shyly. 'I was calling a cab, actually. Last night didn't quite live up to my expectations, so I thought there was no point in sticking around.'

His lips quirked into a sardonic half-smile. 'Not as good as last time? I must have lost my touch.'

Pouring coffee and handing it to him, Kate kept her face completely straight. 'Probably you just need a bit more practice. It's all about training and focus, you see…'

Joking about it was the only way she could think of handling this. She had to keep it light. Casual.

'You sound like Silvio.' He put the cup down and caught hold of her hand, pulling her down against his chest. 'And you seem to know quite a lot about it.'

The musky, masculine scent of his skin made her

feel light-headed with longing. 'Only what you told me last time when I interviewed you.'

He raised an eyebrow. 'I told you about sex?' With one hand he lazily started to unbutton the white shirt. In an instant Kate was drenched with want.

'No,' she gasped. 'About racing. The sex part was more of a…practical demonstration.' His fingers moved downwards, skimming her quivering skin as he slowly undid each button. She gave a breathless laugh. 'It was my first time.'

His hand stilled. Kate felt a tiny prickle of alarm and looked up into his face. His eyes were impossibly dark and utterly unreadable, and although she was still lying in his arms there was something about him that had quite suddenly withdrawn from her.

'In that case I probably owe you an apology.'

'Why?'

He detached himself from her, leaning over and picking up the mug of coffee he'd put on the bedside table a few minutes ago. 'Because I'm quite sure as first times went it left a lot to be desired—emotionally, if not technically,' he drawled.

The sun streaming through the huge window turned his skin to gold and made him seem more beautiful and unreachable than ever. Kate's heart constricted. Sitting up, reaching for her own coffee, she breathed in the fragrant steam for a second and shook her head.

'No. No, it was…' She paused, taking a mouthful

of coffee and hoping it would dislodge the hard lump of emotion in her throat.

This was her chance to try to bring alive some of the magic of that long, deep, breathless night.

But how?

'Well?'

His heavy-lidded eyes were mocking, but she found the laughter that had been bubbling up inside her had vanished and she couldn't joke about it any more.

'It was…special.' She stared down into her mug. Her voice sounded husky with the emotions she was trying to hold back. 'It was *good*. Not just the s-sex bit, but all of it.' She looked up at him, trying to keep the pleading note from her voice. 'Didn't last night make any of it come back?'

'No.'

Aware of the ice in his tone, Cristiano leaned forward with deceptive nonchalance, reaching for a brioche and tearing into it with quiet savagery. He had woken up feeling more at peace than he could remember at any time since the accident, and had lain for a while in the warm, sun-filled room, looking at the majesty of the mountains, his mind going slowly over what had happened.

But it was the moonlight on the snow, the rustle of satin, the taste of salt tears on her skin as he'd kissed her that filled his head. Not the faintest echo of a hot night in Monaco four years ago. No miraculous revelation. No sudden blinding epiphany. Just the same black hole—only now it seemed even darker and more fathomless than ever.

Making a huge effort to keep his voice neutral, he said, 'You'll just have to tell me about it instead.'

'I don't know where to start.'

She sucked a drizzle of honey off the side of her hand. Sitting cross-legged on the bed, wearing his shirt, with last night's make-up smudged beneath eyes that were the same blue as the sky above the mountains, she looked absurdly young and heart-wrenchingly pretty. So much for being plain and boring, Cristiano thought acidly as desire uncoiled inside him again. It would be a lot more convenient if she was.

'How about at the beginning?'

'Well,' she began hesitantly, 'it was a really hot day…'

He needed to know this. It was why he had brought her here, after all, but right at that moment talking or listening were the last things he felt like doing. He shifted onto his side, propping himself up on one elbow and trying to focus on what she was saying instead of on the hardening of his body, the strength of his sudden longing to pull her into his arms again and cover her mouth with his.

'…I'd only found out an hour before I had to leave for the airport that I was coming,' she was saying, in her soft, slightly self-deprecating way, squashing brioche crumbs beneath her thumb as she spoke. 'My boss was supposed to be doing the interview, but his wife had suddenly gone into labour so he had to send me instead. I was terrified.'

'Of what?'

'Of the whole thing—getting on a plane, watching the race, meeting you. Luckily there wasn't too much time to get into a state about it, but there wasn't any time to think about what to wear either. It was raining in Yorkshire, and I thought I ought to look smart and professional, but of course I'd never been to a Grand Prix before.' She glanced up at him with a rueful smile that brought dimples out in her cheeks. 'I put on the tailored grey suit I usually wear to meet new clients. All the other girls were wearing—'

'Hardly anything at all,' Cristiano said acidly.

'Exactly. And they were all so beautiful and glamorous, and I felt so…out of place. Fast cars scare the life out of me anyway, and I was totally unprepared for the noise and the petrol smell and everything. It was all a bit of a nightmare.'

She was talking faster now, her head bent, her hair falling forward and partly covering her face. He wanted to reach over and tuck it behind her ear, so he could see her properly, but didn't trust himself to touch her.

'I watched you qualifying from the balcony of the Campano building,' she went on, 'and then afterwards I went to the press suite to do the interview. Your PA said you'd want to shower and rest for a while first, so I waited. Everyone else had disappeared to a party on some yacht and the place was deserted. When you didn't appear I thought you must have gone with them, and I felt really stupid for waiting like that.' She took a deep breath. 'So I went to look for you...'

She faltered and stopped, seeming to search for words for a moment, before shaking her head and saying nervously, 'But I'm sure you don't want to know all of this.'

Cristiano reached out and took the plate from her crossed legs, placing it back on the tray. The brioche had been reduced to a heap of crumbs.

'Yes, I do,' he said, with quiet irony. She couldn't begin to understand how much.

'I found the room with your name on the door,' she said very quietly. 'You were asleep.'

Cristiano gave a hollow laugh. 'A classic interview-avoidance technique.'

Kate moistened her lips with the tip of her tongue and darted him a quick glance from behind that curtain of honey-coloured hair. Her cheeks were pink.

'The thing is you were really deeply asleep.' Her voice was little more than a whisper now. 'You were lying there, very still, and you hardly seemed to be breathing and...and...I thought you were...d-dead.' She raised her head and looked at him with those luminous blue eyes. 'Ridiculous, isn't it?'

Cristiano was about to make some sardonic remark, but stopped himself when he saw the stricken expression on her face. 'Not ridiculous at all,' he said gravely. He hesitated, and then almost unwillingly found himself continuing, 'When I first started driving my biggest weakness was my inability to concentrate, so I taught myself deep meditation techniques. They helped me to focus, and also to come down from the adrenaline rush after a race because they slow your heart-rate.' Keeping his eyes fixed on hers, he picked up her hand and laid it against his chest. 'Mine is unusually slow to start with anyway...see?'

Her clear eyes widened. Darkened. The room was very still and quiet as the moment stretched and she waited...listening...feeling the beat of his heart.

Which, of course, had accelerated the instant she touched him. *Maledetto*. What the hell was he doing, telling her about his weaknesses anyway? That was the second time he'd let slip something private. He'd be spilling everything before he knew it—all the shameful details of his past.

That at least would bring this thing to a quick and painless end, he thought bitterly, noticing the jump of her pulse beneath the rose-gold skin of her throat. Suki was right. She wasn't his type at all. There was no future in this, and it wasn't fair to let her believe for a second that there was. Later he would mention something about getting her back to Monaco. After he'd found out what he needed to know.

'So, what happened next?' he asked roughly.

She pulled her hand away, curling her fingers and burying them in the folds of his white shirt. She took a quick breath. 'I was feeling for a pulse...and you woke up...and...'

'Let me guess. I took full advantage of the situation?'

She gave a breathy laugh, but there was an edge to it. 'No. You tried. But I...I stormed out.'

'Buon per te.'

'You came after me. It was getting pretty late by then, so you offered to take me back to your house to do the interview.'

'Which is how I managed to scare the living daylights out of you on the way, and then take full advantage of *that* situation,' Cristiano said cuttingly.

It was surprisingly uncomfortable being given an insight into his past mode of operation. Sitting up abruptly he punched a goosedown pillow into shape and leaned back against it, putting a bit more distance between himself and the bit of her bare thigh that wasn't covered up by the shirt.

'It wasn't like that,' she said carefully. 'You cooked dinner for me.'

'Pasta?'

She gave a little indrawn breath and lifted her head. 'You remember?'

Cristiano gave a twisted smile.

'No. It was a race weekend. I eat nothing but pasta.'

'Oh. Of course.'

She got up then, unfurling her legs and wrapping her arms across her body as if she was cold. 'We sat outside, by the pool, and...we talked. I asked you the questions I'd been given.' She walked over to the window and stood there with her back to him, so he had a perfect view of her long legs beneath the shirt. He thought fleetingly of all the enticing, erotic creations of silk and lace and even on occasion leather that women had worn to please him in bed over the years, and wondered why none of them had ever had quite the same effect as this. This girl with skin like cream and her soft voice and her gentle hands.

'Did I answer them?' he asked blandly, making a desperate effort to keep his mind on what she was saying.

She turned round, leaning back against the glass. With the sunlit snow-covered mountains behind her, and the morning sun making her hair gleam, she looked like an advert for some kind of wholesome milk-and-honey-type product. She smiled.

'Not really. Somehow you managed to focus the conversation on me more than you, and I ended up telling you all about my brother and my father. You listened.'

Maledizione.

Of course he'd listened, he thought disgustedly. Diverting the subject away from himself and listening instead of talking was just one of the techniques he'd honed to perfection over the years, and one of the ways he avoided giving anything away about himself. It meant nothing. To him, anyway. To her it had obviously been significant enough for her to think he was worthy of her virginity.

He rubbed a hand over his face, pressing his fingers

into his temple as if he could somehow erase the realisation of what he'd been. Often in the hospital he'd thought that the accident was a punishment for the suffering he'd put his mother through, but now it seemed just as likely to be some kind of divine retribution for the way he'd used people.

Women. So many of them that their beautiful faces, their willing bodies, blurred into one. *Too many to remember.*

Caro Dio, the irony.

Reaching for one of the towels that was folded on the chair beside the bed he got up, wrapping it around his hips as he walked towards her. Suddenly he didn't want to hear any more.

'Kate…'

She lifted her head slightly, meeting his gaze with an expression on her face that was almost defiant. 'It helped,' she said simply. 'To admit how scared I was—how scared I'd always been, of so many things. You told me that a life lived in fear is no life at all.'

Cristiano grimaced. 'And that was the line I used to get you into bed?'

Her shy smile pierced his heart. Or perhaps it was just his conscience. She was blushing again.

'Ah, well…it wasn't bed…'

'Where, then?'

He was standing right in front of her now, close enough to see her pupils dilate and catch the sweet scent of her skin, the musky base note of sex that still clung to her body from last night. The towel around his waist suddenly seemed pitifully, dangerously inadequate.

'The swimming pool,' she said huskily, looking straight into his eyes. She was still leaning back against the huge window, only now she didn't look tense, or cold, or shy. There was something very sensual about her tousled hair, the smudges of kohl beneath her eyes, her sweet, plump lips as she spoke.

'You made me close my eyes and you took my hand.' She reached out and took his hand, lacing her fingers through his. 'And very gently you led me into the water, with all my clothes on, and you picked me up and held me against you.'

Cristiano felt his fingers tighten reflexively around hers, echoing the rest of his body.

'I had never felt anything like your strength,' she went on. 'Your certainty. It made me feel so safe. I wrapped my legs around you and very slowly you peeled off my wet clothes...'

He closed his eyes. For a moment, a dizzying, disorientating moment, he thought he felt the warmth of the water against his skin, the smell of the chlorine, the weight of her in his arms. And then all of that was obliterated by the urgency of the moment. Of wanting her. *Now.*

The towel fell to the floor as he grasped her shoulders and pulled her into him.

A second later it was joined by the white shirt, and then, hoisting her up into his arms, he carried her back to the bed.

CHAPTER SIX

KATE stood in front of the gleaming stainless steel range cooker in a sort of dream, stirring the fragrant contents of a large saucepan with absent-minded languor. The wooden boards were warm and smooth beneath her bare feet and her body ached and glowed. Outside the short February day was fading, and the mountains were ice-blue against the flame-streaked sky—a more gaudy and flamboyant version of the pastel-coloured sunrise.

How could the day have slipped by so quickly? she wondered. A smile pulled at her lips as she realised the answer to that question. They'd spent most of it in bed and time had become meaningless as they'd explored each other's bodies and drifted in and out of sleep. But now she became conscious of the gentle ticking of the long-case clock, and, rather than simply providing a soothing background to her thoughts, it reminded her of reality.

Guiltily she reached for her phone, listening for a moment before she pressed Lizzie's number. From outside she could hear the steady thud of the axe as

Cristiano chopped logs for the fire. A delicious shudder of remembered pleasure rippled up her spine as she imagined the movement of his muscles as he unleashed all that tightly restrained power and strength, and, waiting for Lizzie to answer, she found herself walking towards the window to see if she could catch a glimpse of him.

He had his back to her as he took another big cross-section of pine bough from the haphazard pile and put it down on the deeply scarred cutting block. Kate's mouth dried as she watched him pick up the axe, weighing it between his hands for a second before swinging it down. The wood split cleanly open, showing its pale inside.

For someone so strong he moved with an easy, mesmerising grace. He had been wearing a soft and faded denim shirt, but with the heat of exertion he'd taken it off and tied it around his waist, so that she could easily see the outline of his body beneath his fitted white T-shirt. The palms of her hands tingled as the memory of gripping his iron-hard shoulders as he'd thrust into her came back to her. She'd dug her fingers into his flesh and cried out with—

'Hi—you've reached Dominic, Lizzie and Ruby...'

Kate jumped out of her skin as Lizzie's cheerful answer-machine message cut right through her X-rated reverie, and guilt and shame washed through her. She'd completely forgotten she had the phone pressed to her ear. Unable to form a coherent message, she quickly cut the call and darted back to the stove, just in time to pull the furiously bubbling pan off the heat.

Slipping her phone into the pocket of her jeans, she began to stir the pan again, breathing in the wine-and-herb infused steam and distantly thinking that usually she would be frantic with worry if Lizzie didn't answer, imagining all sorts of catastrophes had befallen Alexander. But it was as if Cristiano's touch had stilled her and some of his strength had seeped into her.

After her attempt to explain the events of that night had come to such a breathtaking conclusion, they had spoken little. Drugged with pleasure and drained from exertion they had simply lain together, and Kate had understood in some deep-down part of herself that if this was all there was, if there was no future for them, the quiet bliss she felt then would last her for a lifetime.

But she wasn't going to think like that. Not yet. She still had this evening…tonight…to help him remember, or to make him feel that way again. To get past the remote, guarded stranger with the expressionless eyes and the cynical smile and find her way back to the man she had got to know that night in Monaco. The man who had told her his secrets and cried in her arms.

It wasn't over yet.

Cristiano stood up, wiping the sweat from his forehead with the back of his hand. He should go in. The low sun had moved around to the other side of the house now, the light was fading, and the heap of logs he had split in the last hour was enough to keep the fire blazing for a month.

In truth there had already been more than enough logs, and although he'd told himself that the least he could do to repay Francine's kindness was build up supplies for next time she visited, he knew that his real reasons were far more selfish.

He'd come out here to try to rouse himself out of the unfamiliar lethargy that had gripped him since they'd arrived last night. He carried an armful of logs around the corner of the house and looked out towards the distant slopes. The dying sun was painting the snow an unlikely shade of orange, and he paused to watch two skiers weave their way down, plumes of white flying up in their wake. Usually he would be desperate to get out and join them, but today, with his body still sated and slow with pleasure, the impulse to throw himself down a black run was spectacularly absent.

It bothered him.

During the endless weeks Cristiano had spent lying on his back in a hospital bed he'd been so restless that the doctors had had to inject anaesthetic into his spine to immobilise him and give his body a chance to recover. Every minute had felt like an hour, and he had vowed then that when he was back on his feet he'd never take it for granted again. Never waste a moment.

And yet this afternoon it had cost him almost as much effort to drag himself out of bed with Kate as it had to get out of the bed in the hospital four years ago. He had never imagined that he would actually choose to spend the best part of a day doing nothing when there was some of the best skiing in the world literally right outside the door.

Although they hadn't exactly been doing nothing, he acknowledged with a sudden shaft of sharp desire, tightening his grip on the armful of logs and heading towards the house. After four years of near-celibacy it was as if he had discovered sex for the first time and was now experiencing it with the hungry, focused intensity of a teenage boy. But with more skill, thankfully. Never before had he lost himself so thoroughly in the simple act of sleeping with a woman, and God knew in the old days he had given himself enough opportunity.

The problem was he didn't want to be lost. He had come here to find his way back.

Kicking the basement door open, he put the logs down and began stacking them in the neat woodpile against the wall. He needed to get back to Monaco. Back into training. Francine's theory had so far failed to deliver, as had his own idea that sleeping with Kate Edwards again might help him to remember.

The reverse was true, he thought despairingly as the pulse of unease that had been beating at the back of his mind all afternoon seemed to get louder and more insistent. It was as if she had some mysterious hold on him, and every minute he spent with her in his arms dragged him deeper into blissful oblivion so that he forgot about things like getting back on the track and pushing himself again. In fact he forgot about everything that drove him. Everything that mattered.

Suddenly he froze, a log in his hand, then swore with quiet brutality as realisation slammed into him like an iron fist. Realisation of what else he had forgotten. Why he was uneasy.

Throwing the log down again, he headed for the stairs.

'That smells good.'

Startled out of her indolent trance, Kate glanced up and felt herself blush—partly at being so deeply lost in thought that she hadn't heard him come in, and partly because standing there in the doorway, with his hands dirty and his hair clinging to his forehead with sweat, he looked so outrageously sexy. She looked away again, turning her attention very pointedly to the saucepan.

'So it should, with a store cupboard like this to cook from,' she muttered shyly, stirring hard. 'Where I come from "essentials" means a tin of baked beans and a packet of cheap chocolate digestives—not organic beef and a complete A-Z collection of freeze-dried herbs. Are you sure it's OK to use all this stuff?'

'I'll replace it all.'

Something about his voice made her look up again, and her heart gave a little skip of foreboding as she noticed the dangerous blankness of his expression. There was a muscle jumping above his jaw.

'Cristiano? Is everything all right?'

He detached himself from the doorway and came towards her, bringing with him a blast of ice-cold fresh air and pine resin. His eyes were the hard, opaque black of marble.

'I just remembered something.'

Kate gave a little hiss of breath.

Cristiano smiled: a hollow, bitter smile. 'Unfortunately I don't mean that I've suddenly undergone a miraculous recovery. Just that I realised—' He pushed a hand through his hair, and for a moment the cold, impassive mask slipped a little. 'The first time we slept together…I wasn't thinking straight. I didn't use protection.'

The room darkened. Heat roared behind her eyes. Kate struggled to keep her breathing normal as Alexander's face swam in front of her eyes. *Oh, God, I must try ringing Lizzie again*, she thought irrationally as a wave of protective love for her son almost knocked her sideways. Leaning against the kitchen worktop, Cristiano's voice reached her from a long way away.

'It might be a good idea if we contacted a doctor for some emergency contraception.'

Kate bit back a burst of hysterical laughter, and was just about to point out that it was a bit late to think about that now when realisation dawned. He wasn't talking about the night four years ago when Alexander had been conceived—what she thought of as the first time they had slept together—but *last night*. The first of the three or four times they'd made love in the last twenty-four hours.

Weak with relief, she picked up a teatowel that had been draped over the bar of the range door and pretended to wipe her hands on it, simply just to have something to occupy them while she composed herself enough to speak normally.

'There's no need. It's fine.' She gave a slightly shaky laugh, 'As long as you're not trying to tell me you've got some terrifying disease.'

'Of course not. I just wanted to know if there's a risk you could be pregnant.'

Risk. The word jumped out at Kate as if it had been written in ten-foot-high fluorescent letters and hung with flashing lights. She was the most risk-averse person she knew, while Cristiano Maresca was someone who courted it, flirted with it. In every area except this one, apparently. He was quite happy taking his chances with death, she thought sadly. But not life.

She shook her head. 'I'm on the pill. I would have said something if I wasn't.' Her hands were twisting the teatowel round and round, tighter and tighter, but she made another attempt at a laugh, trying to make it sound as if the whole subject was a matter of little consequence to her. 'Especially since one of the questions I asked you in the interview we did in Monaco was whether you wanted a son to carry on the Maresca name and reputation. Your answer was a resounding no, so unless anything's changed...'

As she spoke he turned his back and walked across the kitchen, away from her. The clock ticked, marking out the seconds as her fate hung in the balance. *Now!* a little voice in her head cried. *Tell him now!* But words loomed and faded in her head, and none of them seemed to connect up to make the right sentence.

'It hasn't.'

And with those terse, ice-edged words the tentative hope she had carried in the deepest, most secret recesses of her heart was snuffed out. She blinked, trying to swallow the boulder that seemed to have lodged in her throat, glad of the solid wood she was leaning against.

'Look, I've been thinking...I really must get back to Monaco tomorrow.' Her voice sounded a little hesitant, but otherwise astonishingly normal. 'I was wondering if there's a train or something I can get?'

Opening the fridge, Cristiano took out a bottle of champagne. She watched him tearing off the foil with ruthless expert fingers.

'I'll drive you.'

Kate licked her dry lips and looked away. 'Oh, no, really—there's no need for that. You came here to ski.'

He twisted the cork out of the bottle. His eyes met hers over the top of it and he gave a bland smile.

'I didn't, actually. And I need to get back too. Pre-season testing starts soon, and I have to put in a lot of hours on the track before then.'

A shadow passed over his face and he turned away abruptly, opening a cupboard behind him and taking down two crystal flutes. Kate watched him, the constant low-level desire she felt whenever she looked at him now spiked with an unbearable sadness.

'How can you want to do it again? After what happened?'

'It's not a choice,' he said coldly. 'It's just what I do.'

'It doesn't have to be.' Her voice was so quiet that even in the silent kitchen it was almost inaudible.

'Yes, it does.' His face was expressionless again as he came towards her. Leaning past her, he turned off the heat on the stove and took hold of her wrist.

'Come with me.'

'Where are we going?'

'I want to show you something.'

And that was all it took—the low rasp of his voice and the warmth of his touch—to unleash that hot, liquid rush inside her.

Letting him lead her up the stairs, Kate felt bruised and brimful of emotion—so fragile that the slightest touch might make her dissolve. But somewhere she also felt freed. All this time she had been carrying the burden of her knowledge, wondering how to share it with him. By telling her that he still didn't want to be a father he had released her from that responsibility.

For now. The time would come when he would have to know, and she would be able to tell him without emotion or agenda or pressure. But that time wasn't now. Now was for something altogether different.

Shadows sloped across the floor as he led her into the bedroom. She was quivering with want, with need for his touch, but he didn't stop by the bed. Kate felt a stab of disappointment as he let go of her hand and pushed open the doors onto the balcony.

'Close your eyes.'

After the warmth of the house, the frozen air made her gasp. She tensed, trying to hold herself steady against the trembling that gripped her, which was only partly to do with the cold. She heard the clink of glass as he put down the champagne, and then jumped as she felt his fingers—cool from the chilled bottle—close around hers again and draw her forward.

The wooden balcony was icy beneath her bare feet. The bitter air made her cheeks tingle and the inside of her nose sting as she breathed in a great lungful of it. As the darkness swirled behind her closed eyelids every inch of her skin seemed suddenly exquisitely sensitive, brought alive by the sharp cold, the anticipation of his touch.

'OK, you can look now.'

Cristiano's voice beside her was throaty and hushed.

Goosebumps rose on her arms. For a moment she squeezed her eyes shut tighter, wanting to stretch out the magic, make it last for ever.

But nothing lasts for ever, she thought with a barb of sorrow, and opened her eyes.

In the rays of the dying sun the mountains looked like fire opals, as if they weren't simply reflecting the light but had absorbed it and were glowing from within. The sky was a livid slash of orange, overlaid with swollen clouds of purple, black and yellow, like a bruise. It felt as if they were the only people left in the world.

'It's…incredible,' she breathed, turning to look at him.

And then she noticed the square wood-panelled pool built into the balcony just beyond the doors to the bedroom. Steam was rising and swirling in the frozen air from the surface of its azure water. She gasped, bringing her hand up to her mouth as her eyes widened in surprise and delight.

'A hot tub?'

'Yes.' He followed her over to it and wrapped an arm around her waist, pressing his lips to her neck and murmuring, 'Do you want to get undressed before you get in this time? Or would you like me to take you in fully clothed again?'

A huge, shuddering ache of desire went through her, making her slump helplessly against his hard chest. She gave a low moan, tilting her head sideways to expose her neck to the caress of his lips, almost fainting with longing as his hand slipped beneath her loose top and came to rest on her bare midriff.

'We can't undress out here...' she protested weakly. 'We'll freeze....'

His low, sexy laugh sent another tide of slippery lust gushing through her.

'Not if we do it quickly. And I promise you won't feel the cold at all in a minute.'

She gave a high shriek as he took hold of the hem of her top and pulled it swiftly over her head. The cold rushed over her body, stealing her breath, making her breasts throb and her nipples harden and tingle.

Or was that nothing to do with the cold and everything to do with the fact that already Cristiano had undone her jeans and was pulling them down over her hips?

His hands were warm on her thighs, and she could feel the heat from his body radiating against her back. Stepping impatiently out of her jeans, she twisted round in his arms, suddenly desperate to feel his naked skin against hers. Finding his mouth with hers, she pushed up his T-shirt with one hand whilst feeling for the button of his trousers with the other.

The biting cold and the urgency of her need made her clumsy, but he was there, finishing what she'd started, yanking off his own clothes. If her mouth hadn't been locked on his Kate would have shouted with triumph as he stooped and swept her up into his arms. Every inch of her was crying out for him, and as he lowered her down into the silken steaming water she couldn't suppress a violent shiver of bliss.

There was a seat around the edge of the pool, beneath the water. As Cristiano sat on it Kate detached her lips from his and shifted her position, so that she was facing him, straddling his legs, feeling his erection against the softness of her inner thigh.

'Kate...'

She stilled, her breath catching. Behind him the sunset was as gaudy and improbable as a painted ceiling in some baroque temple, and its fiery glow burnished his dark hair and made his beautiful torso look as if it had been cast in beaten copper. His face was in shadow, but his eyes gleamed—dark and liquid with want.

Wanting *her*. Now.

The knowledge was powerful enough, erotic enough, to make her insides tighten with the beginnings of one of the wrenching, devouring orgasms he gave her. She was torn between wanting to impale herself on him, screaming out her joy and need, and wanting to take it slowly, savouring every moment.

There weren't many left, and she would have to feed on them for a lifetime.

Water cascaded from her body as she hitched herself up on her knees, leaning into him, opening up to him. Cristiano's eyelids flickered for a second as beneath the water she took hold of his throbbing erection and held it for a quivering moment, before lowering herself onto him, inch by inch.

Their gazes were locked, mesmerised. Steam curled around them, enclosing them in a hazy, enchanted place that was quite separate from the rest of the alpine landscape with its sharp, clear air. Quite separate from anywhere Cristiano had ever known. His hands held her bottom as her hips moved and her softness enclosed him—hot and tight, her body as wet on the inside as it was on the outside. Her blue gaze closed around him, as warm and silky as the water, sucking him in.

Her fingers dug into his shoulders and her lips parted as he felt the first spasms of her orgasm. It almost undid him, rocking the control that was the foundation of everything he did to its very core. Her eyes slid out of focus and he held her tighter, gathering her closer to him as her head tipped backwards and she gave a shivering gasp.

The convulsive spasms of her orgasm ricocheted through him, pushing him to the edge of a vortex, and the next moment he felt as if he was plummeting downwards, blackness enfolding him, as he spilled into her with a low, fierce moan.

The surface of the water grew gradually flat and glassy again, and the fire in the mountains died and they receded into the night—shadowy icebergs against a starry sky. Cradling her in his arms, Cristiano felt a curious peace. As if he never had to prove anything again. As if he had come home and was the man he'd always wanted to be.

CHAPTER SEVEN

SOMEWHERE a phone was ringing.

Kate's eyes flew open and she sat up, disentangling herself from Cristiano's embrace as she looked around dazedly. It was early—the dirty yellowish light of a sunless dawn filled the room like fog, and beyond the window the mountains were barely distinguishable against the colourless sky.

The phone rang again—a synthesised burst of electronic noise that was made to sound like the ring of an old fashioned telephone. Adrenaline burst through Kate's bloodstream, and her heart was battering against her ribs as she got out of bed, picking up a towel from the floor and wrapping it around her. It was cold and damp.

'What's the matter?'

From the bed, Cristiano's voice was gravelly with sleep.

'My phone,' Kate muttered, rummaging through the clothes in her bag, her trembling fingers tangling in cool blue satin as she searched for it. 'I can't find it.'

The ringing continued, exasperatingly distant.

Getting out of bed in one lithe, liquid movement, Cristiano loped to the doors onto the balcony and pulled them open, letting in a blast of snow and bitter air. For a split second some abstract part of Kate's brain registered the aesthetic perfection of the snapshot image—his warm butterscotch coloured skin standing out against the stark monochrome of the landscape, his sculpted frame every bit as powerful and magnificent as the mountains. And as distant.

He picked up her jeans from the floor, where she had stepped out of them last night. Immediately the electronic noise got louder. Slipping the phone from the pocket, he glanced at the screen before holding it out to her. His eyes were hooded and opaque.

'Someone called Dominic.'

'Oh, God.'

The blood drained downwards, leaving her feel hollowed-out and dizzy with dread. Her hand was shaking so much that it took three attempts to hit the button to accept the call. Muttering vague pleas under her breath, she pressed it to her ear, vaguely aware of Cristiano pulling on jeans and walking past her to the door, but too dazed with alarm to register the careful blankness of his expression.

'Dominic! Is everything—' Her throat was full of sand, and she had to swallow awkwardly before continuing. 'Is everything all right?'

'Kate, sweetheart—now, please don't panic.'

The words were reassuring enough, but the tone in

which he spoke them was anything but. There was no trace of its usual ironic, bantering note, and in its place was a gentle gravity that made the ground tilt beneath her feet.

'What is it?' she whispered hoarsely. 'It's Alexander, isn't it? Is he ill?'

'It's probably nothing,' Dominic replied quickly. 'But he's a bit off-colour. He had a bit of a temperature yesterday, and was complaining of a headache, and then he was sick in the night.'

'Oh…' It was an exhalation of relief. She felt like the damsel tied to the railway tracks in the old black-and-white movies, when the train driver had put the brakes on just in time. 'He'll probably be lots better this morning. Sometimes these stomach bugs are really horrible, but they only last a few—'

Very gently, Dominic cut her off. 'Kate, honey, it doesn't look like it's a stomach bug. We've brought him into hospital just in case.'

'Hospital?' She bit her lip against a whimper of distress. 'Oh, God, Dominic, what for? Please—just tell me what's happening.'

'They're doing some tests…just to be on the safe side…to rule out anything serious.'

'Serious?' Kate echoed numbly. The train was gathering speed again, bearing down on her. 'What kind of serious?'

There was a pause. Wrapped in the damp towel, Kate suddenly realised she was shaking violently.

'Meningitis.'

The room went black. A whooshing sound filled her head. The train hit. She swayed, groping blindly behind her for the edge of the bed.

'Oh, God,' she breathed hoarsely. 'Oh, God.'

'Sweetheart, please—don't panic,' Dominic begged. 'He's completely stable at the moment, and he's in absolutely the right place. Honestly—the doctors are totally in control. It's just a question of finding out exactly what it is so they can start him on the right antibiotics.'

Kate stood up again, staggering forward and starting to stuff the clothes that were spilling out of her bag back in. 'I should be there,' she whispered. 'I have to be with him.'

'Of course. I knew you'd want to be. I've managed to book you on a flight from Nice this morning at nine. That means you're going to have to get a move on, darling. Can you do that?'

'Yes.' The jeans that had been left out on the balcony all night were soaking wet. She bundled them up and shoved them into the bag anyway. 'Nice. Nine a.m. I just have to...' She straightened up, pressing her hand to her head as she remembered the long drive northwards the other night. 'Oh, God, I don't know...'

'Kate, it's going to be fine,' Dominic said firmly, as if he was talking to a child. 'You are absolutely *not* to do your usual "worst-case scenario" on this—do you hear me? Telling you on the phone makes it all sound much worse than it is—you'll see when you get here. Alexander's feeling a bit rough, and he wants his mummy, but he's going to be all right so please, *please* don't worry.'

'No. Right.' Going into the bathroom for her tooth-brush, Kate caught sight of her face in the mirror above the sink. Her eyes were two dark pools in a face that was waxen with horror.

'G-give him my love, won't you?' She watched her bloodless lips form the words. 'Tell him I—'

She stalled as the panic closed up her throat and tears suddenly spilled from her eyes.

'You can tell him yourself in a few hours,' Dominic said gently. 'I'll see you at the airport.'

Nodding mutely, Kate let the phone fall from her ear and closed her eyes as the tears ran down her cheeks. Alexander's face swam in the darkness in her head: his smile, and the way it made dimples show in cheeks that were as smooth and brown as caramel, his dark, dark, expressive eyes...

'Here.'

She jerked her head up and found herself looking straight into another pair of bitter-chocolate-coloured eyes. Cristiano was standing in front of her, holding out a mug of steaming coffee.

'Thank you.' She took it quickly and ducked past him, out of the confined space of the bathroom, and back into the bedroom where she started to pull things out of her bag again, looking for something to wear.

'I have to get home.'

'So I gathered.' He was leaning against the door-frame, his voice cool and neutral.

Kate's teeth were chattering. 'I need to get to Nice airport. My flight is at nine, so I need to check in at eight, which means...' She went to look at her watch, blinking stupidly at her wrist for a moment before she realised she wasn't wearing it.

Picking it up from the bedside table, Cristiano handed it to her. His face was shadowed with stubble, which gave a sexy, dishevelled edge to his beauty—or would have done if it wasn't for the mask-like blankness of his expression.

'Impossible, I'm afraid. We're at least five hours from Nice.'

'But I have to get there,' she gasped, feeling as if she was hanging by the slenderest thread over a vast, dark, churning abyss. 'My *son* is in hospital!'

Her anguished outburst was interrupted by the sound of Cristiano's mobile phone. Answering it, he turned away, talking in husky, rapid Italian that at any other time would have made Kate's blood quicken. Now she could feel nothing but agony at his indifference. Vaguely she wondered if he was talking to a woman—making arrangements for a replacement as soon as she was gone.

This was the man she had left her son behind for, she thought in horror. He had his back to her, his head bent, and as she looked at his broad bronzed shoulders, the clearly defined muscles beneath the satin skin, she felt as if her heart had been torn from inside her and thrown out into the snow. She had known that there would be no happy-ever-after for them, but she'd thought that the last twenty-four hours had brought some sort of closeness between them…

It was just sex, she thought hollowly. And to her that meant closeness, but to him it meant nothing.

She stumbled forward, grabbing her bag and reaching into it for something to wear. Because her jeans were wet, that just left a knee-length black dress that she had brought in case they went somewhere smart for lunch in Monaco. Putting it on, she felt as if she was going to a funeral.

Oh, please, no…

She had to press her hand to her mouth to stop herself crying out as panic winded her. She had to get home. She longed for Alexander with a desperation that felt like knives in her flesh.

Cristiano finished his conversation. She was aware of him turning back to face her, but couldn't bring herself to look at him. Instead she busied herself with putting on the boots she had been wearing when she'd arrived here, beneath the blue satin dress.

It seemed like a thousand years ago.

'That was Suki,' Cristiano said tonelessly from the doorway. 'The good news is that she's arranged a private jet from Lyon airport.'

Kate jerked her head up, not quite trusting herself to have understood what he was saying. 'Wh-what? You mean I *am* going home this morning?'

'The plane will be waiting for you. You'll save time

on check-in, so in the end the journey will probably end up being quicker than it would have been flying out of Nice.'

'Thank you.' It was a cracked whisper. Cautious hope and gratitude were beginning to flutter inside her. 'What's the bad news?'

Cristiano's ironic smile wrenched at her ravaged heart. 'The weather's too bad for a helicopter transfer. I'm afraid I'm going to have to drive you.'

The magnificent flaming skies of last night were a distant memory—like something from a dream. Overnight the weather had done an alarming *volte face*, and the new day was one of dense iron-grey fog that blanketed the mountains and turned the landscape into a gloomy monochrome oil painting.

Not only was it grim to look at, it was lethal too. Cristiano steered the car down the mountainside with rigid, tense-jawed focus. Yesterday's sun had thawed the top layer of snow, which had then frozen again overnight, turning the roads to glass. Not exactly the kind of terrain the Campano had been designed to handle, but with the snow chains it was coping surprisingly well.

Which just went to show that appearances could be deceptive, Cristiano thought bitterly. He'd thought *he* was the one with things to hide, but all the time she had been keeping some fairly major secrets of her own.

'How old is your son?'

She started slightly at the directness of the question. Or maybe it was the tone of his voice, which sounded harsher than he'd intended in the silence of the car.

'Just three.'

'And are you still married to Dominic?'

He was aware of her turning her head to look at him. Glancing across, he saw that her blue eyes were wide and bewildered in her ashen face. 'Dominic? No…God, no, you've got it all wrong. Dominic's not his father, he's my boss, and he and his wife Lizzie are my friends. Their daughter is a similar age to Alexander. He was staying with them while I—'

She stopped, her mouth open, her expression suddenly stricken.

'This isn't your fault,' Cristiano said harshly, wondering why he felt so relieved that this Dominic person wasn't the father of her child. Someone was, and he couldn't think of any reason why the identity of that person should matter to him. It was the fact that she had a child that was important, he thought savagely. The fact that she was a *mother*. You didn't screw around with women who had children. Children meant involvement. Commitment. And he didn't do commitment.

Dio, why the hell did he feel as if he was trying to convince himself?

Automatically he pulled out to overtake the line of cars in front, and made use of the Campano's impressive acceleration. It was only as he roared away that he remembered her fear of speed.

'Do you want me to slow down?'

She shook her head, looking out of the window at the dingy landscape. 'No, please…I just want to get there.' They were lower down now, but the fog still lay heavily—a grimy curtain shutting out the mountains in the distance. The roads were busier now, with people going to work on an ordinary day. Queues of traffic were building up behind unhurried tourists in camper vans.

'It's stupid, isn't it?' Kate said in a low, aching voice. 'I wasted all that time being scared of things that never happened. Plane crashes and freak accidents. I wanted to remake the world for him and make it safe. And now this…' She took a little gasping breath. 'I should have stayed with him. I should never have left.'

The tendons in Cristiano's forearms ached with tension from gripping the steering wheel. 'Don't say that.' The words were forced from between his gritted teeth. 'Guilt just makes everything worse.'

He was aware of her turning towards him again, and had to force himself to keep his eyes fixed on the road ahead.

'What makes you say that?'

'Experience.'

The needle edged round the speedometer. Beside him he sensed her stillness, as if she was hardly breathing, just waiting for him to elaborate. Acid burned in his chest. She'd be waiting a long time—he'd never told anyone about his past, and he didn't intend to start now. His own private condemnation was hard enough to bear, without having the judgment of others to deal with as well.

The wail of a siren cut through his thoughts. Cursing quietly, Cristiano checked the rearview mirror and saw a police car some distance behind, lights flashing as it pulled out to pass the line of traffic and catch them up. He looked down at the speedometer and swore again.

It was a stupid mistake to make. The Campano was ostentatious enough to attract police attention if it was being driven by a ninety-year-old learner. He shouldn't have pushed his luck.

Pulling in to the side of the road, he got out of the car. The noise of the siren whined into silence as the police car came to a halt behind them, but the lights stayed on, sliding crazily over the polished wood of the dashboard. In a kind of frozen stupor Kate watched them until she felt dazzled and dizzy.

From outside she could hear snatches of conversation in quick, fluent French. The ache beneath her ribs flared, and she found herself remembering back to the night in Monaco when, rigid with tension, Cristiano had told her how much he'd hated school, how his lack of academic ability had been an acute disappointment to the mother who had made huge sacrifices to give him an education. She should hear him now,

Kate thought with a twist of black humour. He was brilliant.

Through the square of window she had a view of him from mid-thigh to waist—his narrow hips and the flat, hard-muscled sweep of his midriff. She looked away quickly, her dry throat aching, her hands knotting together in her lap. Through the anaesthetising horror she felt as if her numb body was crying out for him, desperately craving his strength. His certainty and reassurance.

But since he had discovered she had a child he had withdrawn from her completely. For a moment there, when he had said that about guilt, the dying embers of hope had glowed a little brighter and she had thought that maybe he might be going to let her in again. But then he had slammed the door in her face.

She looked down at her hands. Her skin had a greyish tinge, like the landscape around them, as if all the colour and life had been leached from everything. Unconsciously her fingers had slotted themselves together in an attitude of prayer. She squeezed her eyes shut.

Oh, dear God, please let Alexander be OK, she mouthed quickly. *Please let me get to him soon.*

Opening her eyes, she saw that the policeman had bent down and was peering in at her, obviously thinking she was utterly unhinged. There had been a time when all her prayers had been for Cristiano, but that seemed so foolish now. Foolish and selfish.

If Alexander gets better, she added silently, *I'll never ask for anything for myself again.*

She unclenched her fingers, stretching them out until the tendons screamed. What was taking so long? Through the driver's window she could see Cristiano signing something, the muscles in his bare forearm flexing beneath the tanned skin as he wrote with a flourish. Handing the piece of paper to the policeman, he shook his hand.

A moment later the door opened and he got in, bringing the scent of outside into the warm fug of the car. There were snowflakes in his hair. Kate felt a wrench of gratitude and compassion as she realized that he was only wearing yesterday's T-shirt. He must be freezing. Thrusting her hands under her thighs, so she didn't give in to the temptation to touch him, she looked out of her window.

'Was that a speeding fine?'

'No.' The engine fired with an almighty shudder. 'An autograph—and the promise of some tickets for the grandstand in Monaco.'

The next moment the throb of the Campano's engine was almost drowned out by the rising note of the siren starting up. Kate whipped her head round in time to see the police car pull past them and accelerate away. As Cristiano followed, the procession of commuters heading into Lyon, and the holidaymakers with cars laden down with skis and luggage, moved aside to let them past.

They covered the remaining distance quickly, but

the wail of the police siren made coherent thought difficult and conversation impossible. That was probably a good thing, Kate told herself, staring straight ahead with aching eyes. What was there to say now?

At the turn-off to the airport the policeman gave a gloved salute through his lowered window and the car fell away, although the sound of the siren still echoed around Kate's head. Avoiding the queues of cars waiting to get into the main terminal car park, Cristiano took a deserted service road, the roar of the Campano's engine echoing off the warehouses and hangars on either side as they sped towards a high fence topped with barbed wire.

Security guards carrying radios leapt forward to open gates set into the fence. Beyond them, on the tarmac, a small plane waited. Kate felt her chest tighten as if concrete were setting in her lungs as Cristiano drove up to it.

He switched off the engine.

The silence rushed in on her, flooding her head. It was like being underwater. The moment had come to leave him, and there was so much she still had to say. But no time to say it. No words.

'This is it.'

Cristiano's voice was cool and grave. For a few seconds they both sat motionless, not looking at each other. Kate opened her mouth to speak, but then he was opening the door, getting out, and it was too late.

With stiff fingers she fumbled ineffectually at the

doorhandle. She felt paralysed, torn between her desperate need to get to Alexander and her sudden horror at the prospect of leaving Cristiano. Coming around to her side of the car, he opened the door and stood back for her to get out. She did so awkwardly, swaying slightly as she stood up so that he had to grasp her shoulders to steady her.

He let her go quickly. His face was blank, but in that second as the wind caught his hair it was painfully like Alexander's.

Kate stifled a sob.

'Time to go,' he said flatly. A steward was coming down the steps of the plane towards them.

'Can I have your number?' she said desperately. 'I need to see you again, to talk…'

Cristiano took a step backwards. His expression was glacial, haughty, his jaw set hard. He didn't have to say anything. Everything about him screamed 'keep away'.

'I don't think that's a good idea.' He nodded almost imperceptibly at the steward to take her bag from the car. His eyes were dark slits in his hard face. 'It's over, Kate.'

The words sliced into her like razorblades, reducing her faith and hope and her memories of that other goodbye—the one four years ago, when he had told her to wait for him—to bleeding ribbons. Somehow she made it to the steps of the plane without looking back, and it was only as it rose into the leaden sky ten minutes later that the tears started to fall.

Closure—that was what Dominic had told her she needed.

And that was exactly what she had got.

CHAPTER EIGHT

'MENINGITIS is a nasty illness, but the most crucial thing in fighting it successfully is early diagnosis.'

From across the desk, the sister of the children's ward smiled kindly. Kate felt she ought to smile back, or give some kind of reply, but it was taking all her strength just to sit there without howling. Fixing her gaze on the collection of cartoon character badges pinned to the front of Sister Watson's navy blue uniform, Kate tried to concentrate on what she was saying.

'Alex has been very lucky. Thanks to the prompt actions of Mr and Mrs Hill we were able to perform a lumbar puncture and find out what strain of the disease your son has before it got too much of a grip. We've started him on a course of intravenous antibiotics and he seems to be responding well. We should begin to notice an improvement in his condition over the next twenty-four hours.'

The cheerful matter-of-factness of her tone seemed to belong to another situation altogether. In Kate's shocked, grief-numbed mind it seemed to be entirely inappropriate in view of the fact that Alexander was lying in a small room down the corridor, with tubes coming out of his arms and nose, surrounded by machines.

'That's good,' Kate responded weakly.

'Of course it is.' Sister Watson beamed. Her hair was scraped back from a plump, slightly shiny face. 'Alex is a very strong little boy, Mrs Edwards. He must get that from you.'

She was trying to be kind. Encouraging. Positive. It would be rude to tell her how wrong she was, or to snap that he wasn't called Alex. He was *Alexander*—like Alessandro. Cristiano's middle name.

'Not from me. From his f-father.'

A wave of clammy nausea washed over her as she wondered where Cristiano was now, and what he was doing. Sister Watson stood up briskly, signalling that the conversation was over and that she had more important things to do than get involved with the personal dramas of feckless single mothers who left their sick children and disappeared abroad.

'Well, whoever it comes from, it's a very good thing,' she said firmly, bustling round the desk to open the door and guide Kate out. 'He's not out of the woods yet, but there's every sign that he's on the way. And having Mum with him is going to make all the difference. I'm sure he'll come on in leaps and bounds now you're here.'

Kate's boots squeaked on the green linoleum as she walked along the corridor to Alexander's room. From the walls the painted eyes of the Little Mermaid and various implausible-looking sea creatures seemed to follow her, wide with silent reproach.

Dominic got to his feet from the chair beside Alexander's bed as she went in.

'What did she say?'

'That I'm a neglectful mother and if I'd been here earlier he would be much better by now.'

'Kate, don't.' Dominic sighed.

'OK, so maybe she didn't say that exactly.' Kate walked over to the bed, her heart lurching sickeningly as she tried to find a place on Alexander's body where she could touch him without disturbing the jungle of tubes and wires. 'I don't know what she said. Stuff. Words. "Responding well…not out of the woods…" What do those things mean, Dominic? He looks so…' Her voice cracked. 'So…ill.'

'Hey.' Dominic came round the bed and put his arm around her rigid shoulders. 'It's just the machines and things, lovey. He's doing really well. Just look how peacefully he's sleeping.'

He didn't add that Alexander had been screaming the place down earlier, and that it had taken a doctor and three nurses to carry out the lumbar puncture, or that the peaceful sleep was partly due to the morphine drip in his arm. He was shocked by how terrible Kate looked. The doctors seemed to think that Alexander would get through this and recover fully, but Dominic wasn't so sure that the same could be said of Kate. In that black dress, with her ashen face and the deep shadows beneath her eyes, she looked as if someone had already died.

'When did it start?' she rasped through dry lips. 'How did it happen?'

Dominic sighed, going over to the window. 'Just like I told you,' he said wearily. 'He wasn't his usual self when he woke up yesterday morning, but we thought it might just be because he was missing you. But then he said he had a headache, and Lizzie noticed that he had a temperature. We gave him paracetamol, and he perked up a bit, but by bedtime he seemed to be worse again. It was Lizzie's idea to ring the doctor.'

'I tried to phone.' Kate closed her eyes in pain as she had a sudden flashback to the kitchen in the chalet, standing at the window watching Cristiano chopping logs, the phone ringing in her hand. 'I tried to phone last night just to check that everything was OK, but there was no reply.'

'We didn't want to lie to you, but we didn't want to worry you for nothing either. I'm so sorry, Kate, I should have—'

He broke off, rubbing a hand over his face, and for the first time Kate was jerked outside of her own misery enough to notice how tired he looked. His kind, familiar face was pale and unshaven, his hair sticking up where he'd repeatedly run his fingers through it.

Guilt ripped through her.

'Oh, God, Dominic, I'm so sorry,' she moaned,

carefully withdrawing her hand from Alexander through the tangle of equipment and going over to where Dominic stood. 'You and Lizzie have been so good—to have him for me and to go through all this. I can never thank you enough for looking after him and knowing what to do.' She dropped her head. 'It's me I'm angry with. I should never have gone.'

'Was it worth it?' Dominic said after a pause. 'Apart from this, was it worthwhile?'

Kate sucked in a deep breath, feeling lightheaded for a moment as she recalled the bone-melting bliss of being in Cristiano's arms again. The profound, inexpressible wonder of making love with him. The fierce joy of touching his hair, smelling the scent of his skin, listening to his voice—even though what he'd said had only confirmed her worst fears.

'Yes.' Her eyelids flickered for a moment, and then she looked up at Dominic through a haze of pain. 'Because now I know. There's no future for us. There never really was.'

It was almost dark by the time Cristiano returned to the chalet. His whole body ached from nine hours out on the mountains, pushing himself—and his luck— harder and further than was safe or sensible.

The delicious lethargy that had gripped him when Kate was here had disappeared at the same time as she did, leaving him with an edgy restlessness that only adrenaline could calm. Or so he'd thought. However, having spent the day hurling himself down black runs, skiing off-piste in a blizzard, and latterly in the gathering dusk as well, he had to admit defeat.

Walking into the warm house, he breathed in the scent of woodsmoke and the lingering traces of red wine and herbs from the meal Kate had cooked the other night—and was almost knocked sideways by the wave of physical longing that smashed into him.

He had to get away from here, he thought irritably, his battered body protesting as he took the stairs two at a time. There was no point in staying. The relaxing break that Francine had prescribed had ended up being anything but, and he knew he was deluding himself if he thought that his memory was going to come back any time soon.

Or that Kate was.

The thought caught him off guard, and sent another surge of unwelcome lust pulsing through him. He didn't *want* her to come back, he told himself angrily. It was just because he was bored, stuck here with nothing to focus on, getting restless without the routine of training. Because the pillows still smelled of her hair, and the glass she had drunk from in the hot tub still stood on the bedside table and he hadn't spoken to another soul since he'd said goodbye to her.

And because he had never been left before. It was always him that did the leaving.

Impatiently he undressed, stripping off his ski gear and stuffing it back into his bag, collecting up the clothes that lay scattered all over the floor and the end of the bed and the chair by the window. Picking up his dress shirt, he paused, closing his eyes and remembering how sweet and sexy she had looked in it as she'd sat cross-legged on the bed, telling him about the night they'd met in Monaco.

Bundling the shirt up, he shoved it viciously into the bottom of the bag, underneath everything else, almost as if that would help him bury the memory and the ache of unfulfilled desire. Turning round, he surveyed the room, checking to see if he'd left anything.

There was something on the floor, sticking out slightly from under the chest of drawers. Cristiano's head pounded and his stiff shoulders ached as he bent down to pick it up.

A black velvet evening bag.

Perhaps it was Francine's. Although it was unlikely that she'd use anything so formal out here, he thought, unfastening the catch.

Inside was an invitation to the Campano party at the Casino. Cristiano's heart skipped as he realised the bag must belong to Kate. Beside the invitation was another piece of paper. He took it out.

It was a letter. Turning it over, he stared hard at the writing on the front of the envelope.

Cristiano Maresca
Personal and Private.

His heart started to beat faster. For a moment he considered ripping it into pieces, or throwing it into the embers of the fire downstairs on his way out.

The coward's way out, a cold voice sneered in his head. Mother Superior's voice.

Gritting his teeth, he sank down onto the bed and tore open the envelope, sliding the paper out and unfolding it with clumsy fingers.

He was shaking now. It wasn't a long letter, he noted with relief as his eyes scanned quickly over the lines. Kate's writing was neat and confident. *Clever*, he thought with a stab of bitter self-loathing. Pushing the hair back from his forehead, he focused hard on the strokes her pen had made on the paper, forcing himself to look hard at the individual letters. They jumped slightly in front of his eyes, rearranging themselves.

Dai sbrigati, Cristiano! You're not trying!

He let out a low curse, tipping his head back and looking around the softly lit bedroom as if to reassure himself that he *wasn't* back in that classroom, with the Mother Superior standing over him, her cane poised to strike him across the palms of his hands at the next word he got wrong.

Concentrarsi.

Well, he had come a long way since those days, he thought bitterly. He had taught himself to concentrate to world-championship standard. But it had been hard enough to get the words to keep still and to stay in order in Italian. English was another matter altogether.

Dear Cristiano...
I don't know if you remember me...

Kate's voice was in his head as with painstakingly slowness he forced his eyes to move from one word to the next. And suddenly it was as if she was there with him again, smiling that smile that made the dimples appear in her cheeks, looking at him with those gentle blue eyes...

Eyes that would be full of pity and scorn if she really *was* here watching him now, he thought disgustedly, getting abruptly to his feet and tearing the paper in half, and then in half again. He didn't need to put himself through this—didn't need to take himself back to that place with its smell of chalk and pencil shavings and feel again the horror of being exposed as stupid. A failure.

Dropping the torn fragments of paper onto the bed, he strode into the bathroom and turned on the cold tap. His reflection in the mirror above the basin shocked him. He was unshaven and hollow-eyed, his hair badly in need of cutting.

You're a waster, Cristiano. Just like your father. You'll never amount to anything.

His mother's voice this time. He stooped, splashing

icy water over his face. *Gesu,* he was going mad. He really needed to get back to Monaco and training. He needed to get back to being the person he'd worked so hard, sacrificed so much to turn himself into—three times World Champion racing driver. Francine had been wrong—he didn't need to remember, he needed to forget.

Back in the bedroom, he zipped the bag shut and pulled it off the bed. As he did so the torn pieces of the letter fluttered onto the floor like confetti. Impatiently he bent to pick them up, glancing down at the top one as he crossed the room to the door.

He stopped dead, as if he'd just walked into a glass wall. Dropping the bag, he held the fragment of paper in both hands, staring down at it in disbelief as his pulse rocketed and the breath whooshed sickeningly from his lungs.

Ragazzo stupido. Read it again. You've got it wrong.

Scowling, he looked at the paper again, staring hard at each word until he could be sure there was no mistake.

You
Have
A
Son.

CHAPTER NINE

LIFE in the hospital had a completely unreal quality. Kate felt as if she'd been abducted by aliens and taken to a different planet—a parallel universe of hushed voices and sympathetic smiles, of squeaking linoleum and rustling uniforms.

Another day was beginning. Through a gap in the geometric print curtains the light was pearly grey. Distantly she could hear the sounds of the city outside waking up, but she felt a million miles from it. It was amazing how quickly this had become her world, Kate thought dully, flexing her stiff back as her gaze moved automatically to her son. A world which had at its centre the bed in which Alexander lay, and which extended only as far as the strip-lit corridor outside, the nurses' station, and the parents' kitchen and bathroom.

She ventured to those outposts as little as possible, preferring to spend every moment at Alexander's bedside, even when he was asleep. The nurses, her mother, Lizzie and Dominic had all tried to persuade her to go home and catch up on her own sleep, or at least shower and change her clothes, but there was no way she was going to leave him.

Not again.

She blinked, fighting exhaustion as she gazed down on the small body in the bed, and a crushing weight of love and anxiety descended on her like a landslide, so that she had to catch her breath. He was so precious. So beautiful. And, with his dark hair falling back from his forehead and his sweet face serious and remote in sleep, so like Cristiano…

A steel door inside her mind clanged shut, blocking off that forbidden area—but not before a convulsion of pure, hot longing had gripped her, making her insides tighten and her skin tingle. She dropped her head into her hands, pressing her fingers into her eye sockets. God, what kind of mother was she? To be feeling such things when her child lay in a hospital bed? It was bad enough that she hadn't been here when Alexander was taken ill, but to be still thinking—still longing for Cristiano now…

It was unforgivable, and it had to stop.

All that mattered now was Alexander.

She opened her eyes, suddenly aware that the sandpapery rasp of his breathing with which she had measured the hours of the night was quieter now. Panic quickened inside her. His chest, which had previously had to suck and labour for each hard-won breath, was almost still. Getting to her feet, she bent over him, her heart racing as she laid her hand on his cheek. His skin felt cool and the hectic flush was gone. In the grey light of early morning he looked milky-pale...

'Please...'

It was a harsh, dry whisper. Stumbling away from the bed, Kate rushed out into the corridor, terror burning like acid in her veins. 'Nurse... Oh, *please*!'

Her voice echoed baldly off the walls of the starkly lit corridor, and the Little Mermaid stared at her with wide eyes—as if Kate had just shouted a rude word. There was the sound of a chair being scraped back and hurried footsteps. Kate threw herself back into Alexander's room and picked up his limp hand, squeezing it tightly.

'Mrs Edwards, what is it?'

It was Nurse Parks—the one with the dyed platinum-blonde hair and the uniform that looked a size too small. The one who always made Kate feel like an over-anxious geriatric from Planet Weird.

'He's so quiet—he's hardly breathing at all.' Kate's voice broke. 'And he f-feels icy cold...'

Calmly the nurse checked the trace on the machine beside the bed, and then picked up Alexander's other hand, gazing nonchalantly through the gap in the curtains as she took his pulse. After a minute she turned to Kate with a slightly patronising smile.

'He's breathing fine, Mrs Edwards, and he feels cold because his temperature has come down.'

Kate's pent-up breath escaped her in a gasping sob. 'You mean he's OK?'

'Absolutely—and he's sleeping peacefully.' Picking

up the clipboard from the foot of the bed, she scribbled some notes. 'I suggest you do the same. Why don't you go and use the relatives' room?'

Kate was shaking her head before the nurse had even finished speaking.

'No, thank you. I want to stay here.'

Nurse Parks shrugged, tucking the pen back into the breast pocket of her uniform and going to the door. 'Suit yourself, but there's no need. I'll let you know if he wakes up, or if there's any change, but by the look of him I'd say he's definitely on the mend now. He just needs some rest—and so do you. He'll be up and about in no time, and you'll need all your energy to keep up with him.'

'Do you really think so?' Kate whispered. Her throat ached with sudden emotion so her voice came out as a strangled croak.

'Uh-huh. I'd get some sleep while you can.'

Walking back to the nurses' station, Nurse Parks smiled to herself. Mrs Edwards was sweet, but she really needed to get a grip. Sitting down behind the desk, she picked up the cup of tea she'd just made and the romance novel she'd been reading, leafing through the pages and trying to find her place. She'd just reached a really good bit, where the heroine had vowed that she'd rather die than let the gorgeous Italian hero know about the child she was carrying.

That was all very well in books, Nurse Parks thought, stifling a yawn. There was nothing fun about single parenthood in real life—just look at Mrs

Edwards. No—if a gorgeous Italian walked into her own life she'd definitely think twice about sending him packing...

The entry buzzer on the door to the ward made her jump. Spilling her tea, she swore crossly.

'Yes?' she snapped, glancing irritably at the CCTV screen.

'I've come to see Alexander Edwards.'

Her jaw dropped. There, in grainy black and white, stood every female fantasy made flesh. Tall, broad-shouldered, with untidy dark hair falling forward over a face that she would have expected to see on the silver screen rather than a small security monitor in the Children's Ward of Leeds City Hospital. Even over the crackly intercom there was no denying the sexiness of the husky Italian voice

'I'm sorry, but visiting hours don't start until ten,' Nurse Parks stammered, aware that she had circles under her eyes from a long shift, and wasn't wearing lipstick. 'I'm afraid I can only make exceptions for next of kin.'

'I am. Alexander is my son.'

Cristiano had been preparing himself for this moment for the last twelve hours or so—since he had seen the words written on that torn piece of paper. But it was the first time he had said them out loud, and they felt strange on his lips.

My son. Mio figlio.

Head down, he walked towards the desk at the end

of the corridor. The antiseptic smell transported him instantly back to the months he'd spent in hospital after his accident, and he felt sweat break out on his forehead. The blonde nurse who had let him in appeared from the office behind it, hastily pressing her lips together as if she had just put on lipstick. Smiling like an air hostess, she directed him to a room along the corridor to the right.

'Grazie,' Cristiano said curtly, and began to walk in the direction she indicated. Then he stopped and turned back. His throat felt raw.

'How is he?'

The blonde nurse's pink lips spread into a smile. 'He's been pretty poorly, but he's definitely over the worst now. He's a real fighter.'

Cristiano had a curious feeling in his chest—as if someone had reached in and taken hold of his heart. Wordlessly he nodded, and carried on down the corridor.

Throughout the last twelve sleepless hours, as he had driven through an Alpine blizzard and waited interminably for the runways at Lyon to be cleared enough for take-off, anger had burned and pulsed inside him like a fever. But now, as he approached the room where his son lay, he realised it had deserted him. As he opened the door he just felt...

Dio. Dio mio...

It was Kate he saw first, and once he'd seen her he found he couldn't tear his eyes from her. She was sitting beside the bed, her arms folded on its edge and her head resting on them, like a very tired Botticelli angel. Her eyes were closed, but in the dead grey light of the early morning the violet circles of exhaustion beneath them stood out starkly against her bleached skin.

She looked so very weary and anxious and defeated that for a moment he had to grip the doorframe to stop himself from rushing around the bed and gathering her up into his arms. And then he looked at the little boy on the bed.

His chest felt as if it was imploding.

Automatically he felt himself moving forward, so he could see past the forest of wires and tubes to the sleeping child. He was aware of the blood rushing downwards from his head, a roaring noise in his ears as he looked at his son's face for the first time.

It was like looking at himself. Like turning back the clock and seeing himself as a small boy.

Until that moment the strongest emotions he had ever felt—apart from sexual desire—had been anger, frustration, humiliation. Those were the things that had fuelled him as a teenager and driven him to do the things he'd done. Bad things. Dangerous things.

But this…

This blew all of them out of the water.

His fingers burned with the need to touch that smooth skin. It was slightly paler than his, Cristiano observed as a boulder of emotion hardened in his throat, but there was still absolutely no mistaking the boy's Italian heritage. Gently, almost reverently, he reached out his hand and touched Alexander's cheek.

His skin was the softest most miraculous thing Cristiano had ever touched. Like his mother's, he thought with a thud. The child stirred a little, his mouth opening as he gave a gusting sigh.

Cristiano moved his hand away, not wanting to wake him. At the other side of the bed Kate jerked awake. Her maternal senses, on high alert, had set some internal alarm bell ringing, and her gaze instinctively flew to Alexander's face. His head had rolled to one side, so he would have been looking at her if his eyes had been open, but he slept on, his expression utterly peaceful.

Her heart swelled, and for a moment she was so groggy with sleep and poleaxed with love that she didn't notice the dark, imposing figure standing on the other side of bed.

And then he spoke.

'He's beautiful.'

Shock jolted through her like forked lightning. Instantly she stumbled to her feet, her heart pounding.

'Cristiano…what are you doing here?'

Her mind was racing frantically. She could almost feel the adrenaline pumping through her, hot and stinging. It shimmered in front of her eyes like a heat haze as she watched him take a step forward towards the bed.

In the sterile, utilitarian setting of the hospital

his beauty had a terrifying and dangerous edge. His dark hair was dishevelled, curling over the upturned collar of a long black overcoat, and at least two days of stubble shadowed his jaw, but all of that faded into insignificance compared to the white-hot burn of emotion in his eyes.

'I came to meet my son.'

His voice was as cold and brittle as ground glass. Kate felt faint. A primitive drum-beat of panic shook her whole body, while her overwrought, sleep-deprived brain struggled not to give in to the terror that was closing in on her like icy water. Some automatic almost animal instinct to protect her child made her wrench her head up and look him in the eye.

'You have no right to just walk in here…'

'*Don't* talk to me about rights.' His voice was low, but it pulsed with tightly restrained emotion. His lips were pale, tightly compressed, his whole body rigid as though he was desperately fighting to maintain control. 'Why didn't you tell me, Kate?'

'I was going to.'

She was too tired, too shell-shocked by the events of the past couple of days to think of anything beyond the immediate need to defend her corner. Her son. Cristiano's arrival threatened to shatter the fragile shell that was containing her raw emotions and she was horrified by the strength of her longing to throw herself into his arms and let him kiss her into oblivion. She backed against the wall, putting as much distance between them as was possible in the small room and clenching her hands into fists.

'When? He's *three*, for God's sake.'

'*I tried…*'

In the bed, Alexander gave another breathy sigh as he shifted position. As usual when he was waking up his small hand went to the drip in the crook of his elbow and tried to tug it out. Watching him, Cristiano remembered doing exactly the same thing after his accident.

The arrow of agony that shot through his own arm now was far harder to bear than the pain had been then. Because it was his son's pain and he could do nothing about it.

Gritting his teeth, he looked away. Kate had moved forward, murmuring soothingly as she bent to brush the dark hair off the little boy's forehead. The thin, metallic light emphasised the pallor of her unmade-up face, and the lines of anguish etched into it, but in that moment there was something so profoundly, exquisitely beautiful about her that Cristiano's breath caught, and he felt a sensation like hot needles pricking the backs of his eyes.

And then she looked up at him and her expression changed to one of wariness, like a cornered animal.

'Please Cristiano, I—'

'Mummy…'

The soft whimper from the bed made her stop mid-sentence, but the way her eyes widened in panic told him all he needed to know. She didn't want him there.

So much for gathering her up in his arms, protecting her, he thought with savage bitterness. The only thing she seemed to want protection from was *him*.

'I'll go,' he said roughly, stepping backwards towards the door. 'But on the condition that you'll meet me later to talk.'

He thought for a moment that she was going to argue. He could tell that she wanted to. But in the end she said quietly, reluctantly, 'My friend Lizzie is coming in this morning. She can stay with him for a little while. But not long.'

'Mummy…'

Alexander's voice was stronger now, more insistent. He was struggling to sit up. Cristiano felt a visceral pull inside him.

'An hour.'

She nodded quickly, keeping her eyes downcast. 'OK. An hour.'

At the nurses' station on the way out, the blonde who'd let him in was talking to another nurse. They stopped their conversation as he walked towards them.

'You're not leaving already?' the blonde one asked, looking up at him from under mascaraed lashes.

Cristiano managed a hard, twisted smile. 'On the contrary—I intend to be around for a while yet. Perhaps you could give me the name of a hotel close by?'

* * *

Kate stared at herself dismally in the mirror of the parents' washroom.

The fluorescent strip light flickered slightly, adding a further sinister element to the whole 'horror film extra' look she seemed to have inadvertently adopted, mercilessly showing up the greyness of her skin and the grease that darkened her hair. She looked as if she should be the one in the hospital bed, not Alexander.

After a solid few days of sleep the difference in him was nothing short of miraculous. She should be over the moon—she *was* over the moon, she told herself wearily—it was just that his new-found energy brought a whole new set of demands that, in her strung-out and exhausted state, she wasn't coping with very well. At the best of times his attention span was pretty short, but now, excited by the novelty of his surroundings, and bored from spending so long in bed, it was getting increasingly hard to distract him from his mission to yank out his IV antibiotic line and run around.

She'd been glad when Lizzie had arrived—bringing a get-well present of a big, shiny book about racing cars—because it had meant the pressure was taken off her own frayed nerves a little bit. Although it had also meant it was time for her to face Cristiano.

Her reflection in the mirror had turned a sickly shade of khaki now. She knew she ought to change out of the black dress she had been wearing since she'd left the chalet—now crumpled like an old dishrag—and attempt to do something to paint out the purple circles under her eyes, but what was the point?

They were meeting to talk about Alexander, she reminded herself bluntly. She didn't need make-up or attractive clothes to do that. As he'd said before she got on the plane, whatever they had shared in Courchevel was over.

As she came out of the bathroom she was aware of a flurry of activity around the nurses' station. At least five nurses were gathered there—more than Kate had seen in all the time she'd been there—and the hospital smell of antiseptic and floor polish was overlaid with clouds of perfume.

And in the midst of them all, lounging with deceptive nonchalance against the front of the high desk, was Cristiano. He had shaved since she had seen him that morning, but the brooding expression on his face made him look as dangerous and piratical as ever.

She shivered, though whether from fear or desire she couldn't say.

He broke away from the cluster of blue-clad figures when he saw her, moving towards her with menacing grace.

'Ready?'

'Where are we going?'

As they emerged through the wide glass doors into the outside world, Kate was instantly assaulted by the cold wind and the roar of traffic. Her footsteps faltered for a moment, and she had to resist the urge to put her hands over her ears to block out the barrage of noise.

Or bolt back inside.

Or bury her head in Cristiano's broad, hard chest.

Walking beside her, he seemed impossibly tall and strong, and Kate's legs felt shaky just from being near him again. Why did he have to be so horribly attractive? It made everything in this nightmare so much more complicated, so much harder to think through rationally. His arm touched hers and she flinched violently away.

'Relax,' he drawled acidly. 'It's that building over there.' Raising an arm, he pointed across the street to an imposing Victorian frontage several storeys tall. Flags hung above the entrance, and a doorman wearing a dark grey overcoat stood at the top of the steps.

'The Excelsior?'

Her heart plummeted. She had just about been prepared to face him across a table in some busy coffee bar, but the Excelsior was the most expensive hotel in the whole of Yorkshire. And the most intimidatingly exclusive.

'I can't go in there,' she protested, almost colliding with him as he stopped to cross the road. 'Both the bar and the lounge have really strict dress codes, and I really don't think I'm quite—'

All of a sudden it seemed that she was talking to

herself. The traffic had slowed for him, and he was halfway across the road already.

'Don't worry,' he said grimly as she caught him up. 'We're not going into the bar or the lounge.'

'What do you mean?'

'I booked a room.'

'No!' She stopped in the middle of the road, unthinkingly stepping backwards in horror. 'I came here to talk about my son. Did you think it would be that easy to seduce me into doing what you want?'

A horn blared behind her as a taxi swerved to avoid her. Cristiano grabbed her arm, yanking her forward. His face was as hard and cold as marble.

'*Our* son,' he said, with a lethal softness that was totally belied by his iron grip on her arm. 'And I haven't decided what I want yet.'

The doorman eyed her curiously as Cristiano led her up the steps. As the heavy doors swung shut behind them the outside world receded again. The entrance lobby was hushed and opulent—like a gentlemen's club, Kate thought, looking nervously around while they waited for the lift, hoping someone else would appear so she didn't have to share it with him alone.

The doors slid open. It was empty.

Casting one last desperate look around, Kate stepped in after him, pressing herself against the wall furthest away from him. Neither of them spoke. Why did all lifts have to have mirrors inside? she wondered miserably, trying not to notice the contrast between her hollow-eyed gauntness and his ravaged beauty. He looked exhausted too, but the difference between them was that he could still stop traffic—literally, as she'd just discovered. She just looked like a road accident.

Her stomach lurched as the lift came to a standstill. Her thoughts raced, but like a cartoon character running over the edge of a cliff they led nowhere, leaving her waiting for the moment when she would simply plunge through thin air and crash to the ground. *I haven't decided what I want yet*, he'd said. What did that mean?

'After you. It's the room right at the end.'

She was shaking as she walked along the thickly carpeted corridor with its endless rows of doors. His hand was perfectly steady as he slid the key card through the reader.

The room she walked into was ridiculously grand, decorated in the same ostentatiously opulent Art Nouveau style as the hallway downstairs. Its antique furniture gleamed in the light of the lamps that stood on every surface, and the warm air was heavy with the slightly sickly scent of lilies and freesias from the huge arrangement on the table by the door.

Against such polished opulence Kate felt more faded and tattered than ever.

'So…' she whispered, touching the fleshy petals of a lily and keeping her eyes fixed on its freckled throat—anything to avoid looking at Cristiano, or at the huge and decadent bed behind him. 'Let's get this over with. What do you want to know?'

'Not yet.'

He advanced towards her. His face was unsmiling and inscrutable, his eyes narrowed as he took hold of her wrist.

Kate made a sound that was somewhere between a gasp and a whimper as ten thousand volts of electricity shot through her already shredded nerves. A torrent of desire instantly gushed down inside her, followed by an acid wave of shame.

'Cristiano, please,' she croaked, pulling her hand away and shrinking from him. 'I can't... I don't want to...I mean—please...I thought you just wanted to talk.'

He could shatter her brittle defences into splinters of matchwood with just one kiss. She knew that. And she hated herself for it.

He jerked away from her, his eyes blazing with a cold fury. 'I do. But you're not in any fit state to discuss anything at the moment. We can talk later.' Stepping past her, he pushed open a door to the right, his movements taut with restrained aggression. Scented steam curled around her, and she found herself looking into a beautiful marble-floored bathroom. In the centre stood a vast Victorian bath, steam rising gently from its surface.

Irrational tears stung Kate's eyes as she realised how badly she'd misread the situation. He had done the last thing she'd expected, and the thing she most wanted and needed at that particular moment. She swallowed painfully.

'But I only have an hour.'

'Today, maybe. But there's always tomorrow, the next day, next week. I can wait.'

Shutting the door behind her a second later, she leaned against it and closed her eyes, waiting for the frantic rhythm of her pulse to slow. She couldn't help but wonder whether what he said was meant as a reassurance or a threat.

Cristiano poured himself some coffee from the silver pot brought by Room Service and looked down onto the street below. A selection of newspapers lay neatly folded and untouched on the edge of the linen-draped tray, and behind him the bathroom door remained firmly shut. As it had been for—he checked his watch—just over half an hour now.

One fingertip drummed an impatient rhythm on the rim of his coffee cup. She'd been so tired—what if she'd fallen asleep in the bath?

An image rose up in his mind of her naked body, glistening with the scented oil he'd poured into the bath, sliding beneath the water, her bruised eyes closed. Impatiently he dismissed it as nonsense, but it was replaced by another image—this time of her in the hot tub in the chalet, her skin glowing in the fiery sunset, droplets of water running down her throat and onto her breasts as she tipped her head back to drink champagne...

Instant arousal hardened his body.

He wanted her. He wanted her as much now as he had in Courchevel, and the fact that she was the mother of his child only seemed to have added a kind of fierce intensity to his hunger. A hunger which she obviously no longer shared. His teeth came together in a taut grimace as he remembered the way she had shrunk away from him, flinching if he inadvertently touched her, looking at him as if he was some kind of dangerous criminal.

She was an entirely different woman from the one who'd sat on the bed dressed in his shirt and talked to him in her soft, musical voice. The one who'd cooked dinner and then left it to go cold while she abandoned herself to passion, arching her back and crying out as she came, so that her voice echoed off the mountains.

The bathroom door opened.

Cristiano took a gulp of scorching coffee and set the cup down, using all his powers of mental self-discipline to refocus his thoughts and gain control of his body as he turned round to greet her.

'Come and have some breakfast.'

Somehow he managed to keep his cool smile in place. The huge hotel bathrobe seemed to swamp her. With her newly washed hair slicked back from her forehead and her face scrubbed clean she looked incredibly fragile.

'I haven't got much time.'

Cristiano poured a second cup of coffee and pushed

it across the polished surface of the table. 'You have exactly twenty-three minutes. I won't keep you any longer than that.'

He couldn't quite keep the edge of bitterness from his tone, and as she picked up the cup and looked at him over its rim he saw anguish flare in her eyes.

'How did you find out?' she said in a low voice, picking up a croissant.

'You left the bag that you had at the party in the chalet. There was a letter inside.'

Stopping in the act of spearing a curl of butter from the silver dish, she looked sharply up at him. 'You had no right to—'

'What?' Frustration made him cruel. 'Read it? It was addressed to me, so I don't think that's technically true. The question is, why didn't you give it to me? Or even better—' he gave her a twisted smile '—tell me what it said to my face?'

Around the handle of her knife, her knuckles were white. For the barest moment her dark lashes swooped down, shuttering off her blue gaze for a second before she looked up at him again.

'I was going to. I wanted to. That's why I came to Monte Carlo—to the party. But you didn't even recognise me.'

His jaw was so tense he had to force the words out through gritted teeth. 'That was hardly personal.'

'I know,' she said softly, spreading butter on the croissant. 'But by the time I found that out I'd already realised that you were different.'

'How do you mean *different*?'

Her skin had been slightly flushed from the bath, but now the colour deepened, concentrating itself into two patches on the apples of her cheeks. Her eyes met his, their clear blue depths shadowed.

'Harder. Colder. More ruthless.'

Cristiano leaned back in his chair, dragging his gaze away from her face and fixing it on the office block on the other side of the street.

'You flatter me,' he drawled. 'The truth is I've always been like that.'

For a long moment she didn't say anything, though out of the corner of his eye he saw her shake her head, slowly and deliberately.

'Not really.' There was a note of sadness in her voice. 'Not underneath.'

Adrenaline leapt through his system, making his vision darken for a second as his head filled with a thousand stinging responses to that utterly misguided statement. *Gesu,* if only she knew what he was really like underneath she wouldn't want to be his bowling partner, never mind the mother of his child.

'If you thought that, why did it take you so long to get in touch?' he demanded scathingly.

'I had tried before. When I was a few months pregnant I came to Monaco, thinking I'd be able to see you and tell you.' The croissant still lay untouched on her plate, and she was holding the knife in her hand, turning it over and over. Twisting it, he thought with a flash of bleak humour. 'Stupid, wasn't I? For two days I stood outside the hospital with all your other fans, waiting to catch a glimpse of your PA or your team boss on their way in or out. I even humiliated myself completely by giving my name to a security guard in the hope that you'd left instructions for me to be allowed in. The man almost laughed in my face.'

'I'm sorry.'

'I left a letter at the hospital before I went home, and I wrote again when Alexander was born, and sent it straight to your house.'

'My PA handles all my post,' he said flatly, getting to his feet. Time was running out, and he knew that he had to keep his promise and take her back to the hospital soon. Running a restless hand through his hair, he tried to keep the impatience from his tone. 'Why didn't you tell me when we were at the chalet?'

She stood up too, raising her chin and saying defiantly, 'Because I realised very early on that it was useless. You don't want a family—you said that yourself. And although I knew that was true when I met you, I hoped I might have been able to change your mind.'

'To change me,' he said bitterly. 'All the time we were together you were testing me, privately making up your mind whether I was good enough to be allowed into my son's life.'

The simple truth of that hit him with all the force of an express train, knocking the breath from his lungs.

She had judged him and found him lacking. And the thing was, he couldn't blame her.

He remembered her telling him of her question about wanting a child to carry on the Maresca name and reputation, and knew exactly why he would have answered it so unequivocally. He knew only too well how futile it was to place any expectations on your children—how cruel it was to make them carry their parents' dreams.

She shook her head vehemently. 'That's not true. I didn't want to put you in a position you clearly didn't want to be in. I didn't just want Alexander to have a father. I wanted him to have a *family.*'

There was something unbearably touching about the way she said it. Cristiano got to his feet. Frowning, he looked out of the window.

'He still can.'

There was a small silence. On the street below a siren wailed.

'How?' she asked quietly. 'What are you saying?'

Cristiano turned back to look at her, keeping his expression neutral. 'That we can give him that. I'm asking you to marry me.'

CHAPTER TEN

MARRY ME.

On paper, those words coming from the beautiful lips of Cristiano Maresca should have made her want to scream with joy and throw herself into his arms. They should have made her yell *yes* without a moment's hesitation, and have her running to the nearest bridal shop to lose herself in racks of ivory satin and lace.

She opened her mouth, but no sound came out.

'Well?'

Cristiano's voice was cool and almost mocking. Which said it all, really.

'Marry you...' she echoed hollowly, staring up at him in disbelief. 'As in properly...for real?'

'Is there any other way to get married?'

'I don't mean that. I mean...'

'To have and to hold, from this day forward,' he said scornfully. 'If you're asking if it'll be some kind of fairytale happy-ever-after, then the answer to that is probably no. I'm not talking about the soft focus bit at the end of a romantic movie. I'm talking about

providing Alexander with a stable base, security—
two parents living under the same roof, bringing him
up together.'

Security. Together. Like arrows, those words went
straight into the heart of her. The man she'd loved
with every beat of her heart for four years was standing in front of her, offering the things she'd always
craved.

Or some of them, anyway. The kind of marriage
he meant seemed to have one or two significant ele-
ments missing.

'To have and to hold from this day forward?' she
whispered hoarsely, getting to her feet and tucking
her hands down into the pockets of the voluminous
robe. 'But what about the other things, Cristiano?
What about forsaking all others? Are you going to
give up your one-night stands with the paddock club
hostesses and the PR girls?'

'That would be up to you. It depends what kind
of marriage you want it to be. I can't live like a
monk.'

'So sh-sharing a bed would be part of the deal?'

'Only if you wanted it to be.' In contrast to her, he
sounded completely offhand, as if he was discussing
some trivial aspect of his Clearspring sponsorship. 'I
may be guilty of many things, but forcing myself on
an unwilling woman isn't one of them.'

Kate didn't imagine for a moment that it was a
situation he'd ever encountered.

He took a step towards her, brushing a stray strand

of hair off her face with a fingertip. '*Do* you want it to be part of the deal?' he asked softly.

'No!' His touch scorched her, bringing her back to her senses. This was exactly what she'd been afraid of. What she'd vowed to avoid. Backing away from him, she raised her head defiantly, pulling the robe more tightly around her. 'Thank you for your offer, but the answer is no. When I get married I want it to be for the right reasons. For *love*, not for practicality.'

His lip curled in a sneer of disdain, as if she'd just said something unbelievably childish. 'In that case I'd better get in touch with my solicitor to work out some kind of formal arrangement for me to see Alexander.'

He pronounced it *Alessander*, Kate noticed distantly. A mixture of Italian and English—which was what Alexander was going to be from now on. A child with two homes, two lives. Two parents—but not in a good way.

'Is that really necessary? You'll be going away soon—back to M-Monaco, or wherever, to race.'

It was a long shot, she knew that. But she also knew how deep Cristiano's passion for racing went. It was her best hope.

'Of course.' He shrugged. 'I'm a racing driver. But that doesn't mean I can't be a father too.'

'But what kind of father?' Inside the pockets of the robe Kate's fingernails were digging into her palms. She felt as if she was pleading for her life. 'What kind of security can you give a child when you put your neck on the line for a living?'

His eyes narrowed. 'What exactly are you afraid of, Kate?'

She gave a humourless laugh, as if to acknowledge that she understood how stupid it was going to sound. 'That he'll just get to know you and he'll lose you.'

Cristiano's voice was ominously quiet. 'So you think he's better off not knowing me at all?'

'Yes.'

The smile he gave her was chilling. 'You don't know what it's like not to know your father.'

'No,' Kate gasped, struggling to hang onto her last shreds of control. 'But I know what it's like to know him and adore him and think he's invincible, and then to have him snatched away from you like *that*!'

She snapped her fingers, blinking back tears. Her breathing was shallow, her chest rising and falling rapidly beneath the robe. By contrast he was glacially calm.

'Even more reason to get some formal arrangement in place, then.'

Kate took in a deep breath, holding it for a second until her lungs burned. Then she let it out slowly, trying to steady herself for a last attempt at reasoning with him.

'Please, Cristiano. Think about it. You can't just walk into his life and then disappear again. It wouldn't be fair on him.'

Cristiano looked at her. Her hair was almost dry now, and in the weak sunlight it gleamed like spun gold. Distantly he was aware of a steady pulse of desire, but desire he could deal with. It was the complicated mix of emotions that this girl seemed to arouse in him that was far more problematic.

His solicitor was excellent. He could hand the matter over to him and keep emotion out of it entirely. It was a legal matter. A matter of rights.

Wasn't it?

Suddenly he was aware of how long it had been since he'd last slept. 'I think you mean,' he said tonelessly, 'it wouldn't be fair on *you*.'

'What are you trying to say?'

'You want him to yourself.'

'No, I—'

'I'm not criticising you, Kate,' he interrupted wearily. He was too tired to play games any more, and the issue at stake was too important. He'd never really given much thought to the idea of having a child, his own miserable childhood having made him feel that it wasn't something he'd want. But now it had happened, he realised he did. Very much. 'I'm not blaming you—you've done this on your own for three years and it can't have been easy. I just want you to know that I'm not going to go along with it either. I'm not going to walk away. So now, when you're dressed, it's time to go back to the hospital. I'd like to meet my son.'

'I don't want him to know who you are yet,' Kate said in a low voice as they waited to be let back in through the security door to the children's ward.

Cristiano looked down on her, one eyebrow arched in sardonic enquiry. 'Do you mean that I'm a racing driver or his father?' he asked blandly. 'I can't decide which you think is worse.'

'Both, now you come to mention it. But I meant that I don't want you to tell him you're his father. It's too soon. Too sudden. Especially when he's been ill.'

A voice crackled over the intercom, telling them to go in. Kate kept her eyes fixed straight ahead as they walked along the corridor—outwardly like two ordinary parents going to visit their sick child together. Her heart was beginning to beat uncomfortably hard at the prospect of what lay ahead.

As they passed the desk Kate noticed that the two nurses who, a moment before had had their heads bent together over a file of notes looked up, mouths open, their eyes following Cristiano as if they were a couple of starving stray dogs and he was the butcher. Irritation fizzed inside her.

'He's also quite shy with people he doesn't know—particularly men—so don't expect too much,' she snapped.

The door to Alexander's room was in sight now, and as they got closer she quickened her steps, feeling a strong urge to run ahead along the corridor and gather him up into her arms, holding him tight so that no one could take him away from her.

'I won't.'

She reached the doorway a little before Cristiano.

Alexander was sitting up, and he and Lizzie had their heads bent together over the racing car book which lay open on the bed. Some of the machines had been taken away, Kate realised, and the room looked bigger, less alarming.

Lizzie looked up as she came in.

'You're back!' she said, her face breaking into a smile. 'And you look *so* much better! How did it—?'

She stopped abruptly as Cristiano appeared in the doorway. Her eyes widened.

'Lizzie, this is Cristiano Maresca. Cristiano— Lizzie Hill.'

He moved forward, his hand outstretched, his face perfectly grave except for a faint smile.

'*Molto piacere*, Lizzie.'

Lizzie was blushing, Kate noticed disgustedly. Confident, sassy, in control Lizzie had fallen instantly under Cristiano's spell just like everyone else, and was blushing like a schoolgirl. Luckily Cristiano turned his attention to Alexander before she actually swooned.

'And you must be—'

Alexander was looking at him steadily with dark, unblinking eyes. Before Cristiano could finish he said, very clearly, 'Man in the car.'

Kate went over to the bed. 'What's that, sweetheart?'

Alexander kept his eyes fixed on Cristiano, as if

he expected him to disappear at any moment. 'Man in the car. In my book.'

Kate opened her mouth to speak, but shut it again. She wasn't sure that either of them would hear her anyway. Alexander was still staring up at Cristiano with solemn, fascinated eyes, and Cristiano was looking right back.

The expression on his face took her breath away.

'I'm Cristiano.'

'From the car. See...?' Dropping his gaze, Alexander began turning the pages of the book Lizzie had brought him until he came to a huge photograph, spread across two pages, of a green sports car. The driver was quite clearly Cristiano.

Cristiano lowered himself gently onto the edge of the bed, leaning in to see the book. Kate turned away, closing eyes that stung with sudden tears, but the image of the two dark heads so close together seemed to have burned itself onto her retinas.

Oh, God—this was what she had wanted, wasn't it? So why did it hurt so much?

'Yes, that's my car.' The deep, dark Italian voice reached her through the darkness like a caress. 'Do you like cars?'

'Yes,' Alexander said quickly. Kate opened her eyes in time to see him reach for the red car Dominic had given him for Christmas from on top of the bedside locker. 'I got lots of cars. This is my Spider.'

Very gently Cristiano took it from him, holding it in his beautiful brown hand. Turning it round reverently, he examined it for a long time. Kate and Lizzie were both watching, spellbound. '*Magnifico,*' he said gravely, handing it back. 'I wish I had a Spider.'

Alexander took it, an expression of fierce pride on his face. 'What car do you have?' he asked.

'A Campano. At the moment I have the new CX8. I've been testing it.'

His eyes met Kate's, and a meteor shower of dazzling sensation exploded in her pelvis.

On the bed, Alexander gave a little bounce of excitement. 'Can I go in it?'

There was a pause. Kate seemed to have forgotten about breathing. Cristiano's gaze was still holding hers, and the intensity of unreadable emotion in it made her feel as if she wanted to shield her eyes. It was such a contrast with the remote, businesslike stranger in the hotel that for a second she felt hope leap inside her.

And then he was turning away, back to Alexander, a slow, heartbreaking smile spreading over his face.

'Yes,' he said, his voice a deep rasp. 'Yes, of course. If your *mamma* says you can. When you're better.'

'Can I, Mummy? Can I? *Can I?*' Alexander piped, looking up at her with his face alight with excitement.

And in that moment Kate understood that she had lost him. Or rather that there had been a part of her son that had never been hers.

CHAPTER ELEVEN

'AND so I thought I'd leave Dominic and join the Moscow State Circus as a naked trapeze artist. What do you think?'

'Hmm. That's good.'

Dully, Kate pushed a mass of pulped tomatoes through a sieve to get rid of the pips. Making soup had seemed like a good idea when she started, but somewhere along the line she seemed to have lost interest. Or energy. Or both.

From the next room the theme tune to one of Alexander and Ruby's favourite television shows started up. Lizzie got up from where she'd been sitting at the table and came to stand beside her.

'OK. I'll try not to take it personally that you haven't listened to a word I've said for the last half-hour. The kids are going to be glued to the television for the next twenty minutes, so how about you stop doing that and tell me how you are?'

Kate looked up, blinking. 'I'm fine.'

Lizzie raised her eyebrows sceptically. 'Come off it, Kate. Since Alexander came out of hospital you've been like a cat on hot bricks, which is perfectly un-derstandable given what you've been through.' She set her mug down on the draining board with a sigh. 'I just wish you'd talk about it, though. Dominic and I are worried about you.'

Where have I heard that before? Kate thought sourly. The new, bitter and twisted Kate Edwards who had taken over the body of the old one couldn't quite forgive Lizzie and Dominic for starting all this in the first place. If it hadn't been for their concern last time, life would be carrying on as normal now.

'You mustn't worry,' she said wearily to Lizzie. 'I'm worrying enough for the whole of Yorkshire at the moment.'

'About Alexander?'

'Mostly. I keep checking him for signs of a fever or mystery rashes. I go in and check if he's breathing several times a night.'

Lizzie made a sympathetic clucking sound and laid a hand on Kate's arm. 'That's entirely normal after he was so ill. And of course the situation with Cristiano doesn't help. Have you heard from him since he went back to Monaco?'

Kate flinched. 'No. And as the Grand Prix season is about to start I'm not expecting to hear anything for months. I half expected a letter from his solicitor, but maybe the fact I haven't had one means he's lost interest in being a father.'

Oh, dear, was that sour voice really hers? She clamped her mouth shut against a further tirade of bitterness and focused instead on the red pulp in the sieve, mashing it with extra force.

'I don't think so. He was obviously knocked out by Alexander, but he must be very busy with training,' Lizzie said soothingly. 'Being a racing driver is a pretty full-time job.'

'Try explaining that to Alexander when he asks fifty-seven times a day when Cristiano is coming to take him out in his car.'

There was a knock at the door. Wiping her hands on her jeans, Kate went to open it, catching sight of her pale, pinched face in the hall mirror as she did so. *God, I look like a ghost,* she thought despairingly. This morning, knowing Lizzie was dropping in and not wanting to face another barrage of concerned questions, she had at least forced herself to wash her hair. It was just a shame she couldn't wash the dark circles away from under her eyes as well.

Another loud knock at the door made her jump. It was probably her mother. Arranging her face in what she hoped was the normal expression of someone who was perfectly happy and coping fine—although she wasn't sure she knew what that was any more—she opened the door.

There, standing on the pavement, his dazzling dark beauty looking utterly out of place against the greystone drabness of Hartley Bridge, stood Cristiano.

Her heart stopped. Her mouth opened, but under his lazy, mocking gaze she found it was impossible to speak.

He, of course, didn't have any such difficulty.

'I've just driven for fifteen hours to get here, so please don't tell me this is a bad time to call.'

His voice was husky, intimate, caressing. Kate felt the colour surge upwards into her cheeks as her stomach imploded with shameful want.

'No, of course not,' she said hoarsely, stepping aside to let him come in.

He didn't get the chance. Alexander, coming into the hall to see who it was, had spotted him. Hurtling past Kate, he threw himself forward and Cristiano scooped him up in his arms.

'*Cristiano!* You came back! Did you bring your car?'

'Absolutely,' Cristiano said gravely, turning around. The dark green sports car that Kate remembered from Courchevel was parked at the kerbside a little way along the street, looking as incongruous as a sabre-toothed tiger in a petting zoo. 'I drove it all the way back from France so you could see it.'

'*Wow!*'

'We're going,' Lizzie whispered, giving Kate a hasty peck on the cheek and a meaningful look as she slid out of the door with Ruby—protesting hotly at being torn away from the television—wriggling in her arms. 'Call me later.'

Cristiano set Alexander down, caught off guard by a sharp pang of reluctance to let him go. The drive through France had cut badly into his training schedule and cost about as much in petrol as the hire of a private jet, but it had been worth it, he acknowledged, watching Alexander approach the car. He stopped a few feet from it, his mouth slightly open, his eyes wide with wonder as he slowly looked it over. Smiling, Cristiano turned to Kate.

Instantly he felt the smile fade.

She was standing in the doorway, leaning against the frame, the expression on her face unbearably sad. She was wearing faded jeans that clung to her long legs and some kind of long-sleeved T-shirt thing in soft, faded cotton. Although from the way Cristiano's body was responding to seeing her again she might as well be wearing a black lace basque and crotchless panties.

'How is he?' he asked gruffly.

'He's good.'

'And you?'

'I'm good too.'

She didn't look good, he thought. She looked as if she needed to be put to bed and allowed to sleep for a week. It was a noble sentiment, although he wasn't entirely sure he'd be able to follow it through.

Alexander was jumping up and down on the pavement, his eyes shining with excitement. 'Can we go in it? For a ride?'

'Of course. Where would you like to go?'

'To the seaside!'

Stepping forward quickly, Kate deliberately avoided looking at Cristiano.

'Come in now, Alexander. It's too cold for you to be

outside without a coat,' she said, hating the miserable, impatient note in her voice, and the way Alexander's little face fell as he did as he was told, casting a final covetous glance over his shoulder at the car as he took her hand.

Why did Cristiano Maresca seem to have a knack of turning her into someone she didn't want to be?

He caught hold of her elbow as she turned to follow Alexander inside, pulling her back so that they were both in the tiny porch. He seemed to fill it right up.

'What's the matter?' His eyes were opaque. 'You don't like the idea?'

'Can you even get a car seat in that thing? Because there's no way—'

'Relax, *carina*. I took the precaution of buying one to fit in case the one you had didn't go in. So if that's all…?'

'It's too far,' she muttered, mustering all her defences against the onslaught of his nearness. 'And too cold. He's not well enough yet.'

Cristiano's eyes narrowed. 'I thought you said he was better?'

'He is, but still—a whole day out, and you hardly know him. What would you do if he was ill? If he was sick in your lovely car?'

'Hmm… Honestly?'

A faint smile touched his lips. Kate raised her chin, desperately trying not to let herself notice—his lips or the smile.

'Yes,' she said stiffly.

'Get you to deal with it?'

'Me?' she gasped. 'But—'

'But I'm sure the situation won't arise,' he said softly, taking hold of her shoulders and steering her back into the house. 'Alexander seems fine. Now, go and get whatever you need for a day at the beach in your freezing English weather and let's get going.'

It was the kind of bright, blue-sky March day that from behind glass looked as if spring had arrived. The North Yorkshire Moors were a vivid patchwork of emerald-green and brown and purple as the wind chased cottonwool puffs of cloud across the huge, wide sky.

Sitting in the now-familiar passenger seat, Kate felt strangely numb. She had come full circle, she thought sadly. Often over the last four years she had congratulated herself on how much she had changed, matured from the tight-lipped, frightened girl who had first got into Cristiano Maresca's car and sat petrified while he drove La Grande Corniche.

And yet here she was. More tight-lipped and frightened than ever.

In the back seat Alexander had started the journey in a state of high alert, sitting bolt upright in the new car seat, his head turning as he looked out at all the people who turned to stare at them as they roared up the high street in Hartley Bridge. But it was when they had got out onto the road over the moors that he had loved it most, when Cristiano had pressed his foot down. Alexander's squeals of delight had been drowned out by the throaty roar of the engine as the car had leapt forward. Now he was in a kind of trance of happiness, looking out of the window for the first glimpse of the sea.

Kate glanced across at Cristiano, still not quite able to believe that he was really there. 'I thought the Grand Prix season was starting soon,' she said awkwardly. 'I didn't think I'd see you until it was over.'

He looked at her thoughtfully. 'For a moment there it sounded like you missed me.'

Heat tingled into her cheeks again. No danger of anyone mistaking her for a ghost when Cristiano was around, she thought miserably. A tomato, perhaps...

'Yes, well, Alexander's been asking for you.'

'I came as soon as I could.'

If she'd been hoping that he would elaborate on what he had come for, or how long he was staying, she was disappointed. Silence fell again.

'How did your training go?'

Cristiano hid a wry smile. 'OK.'

It wasn't training, it was pre-season testing—as every one of the women he had slept with in the past would have known. Along with his exact lap times too, probably. The newest Campano model had caused quite a stir. From the moment Crisitano had got into the driving seat it had felt inexplicably right, and once he'd got out there on the circuit the demons that had dogged him since the accident had fallen away, and he had delivered a lap time that had made headlines on all the sports pages and several front pages as well.

No flashbacks, no panic attacks. Maybe Francine's unorthodox treatment had worked after all.

Or maybe it had had nothing to do with Francine and everything to do with the woman beside him.

He'd got Suki to send Francine a case of vintage Krug anyway, but when he had tried to think of something to buy for Kate he'd been completely stuck. The gifts he usually bought for women—perfume or designer underwear, the odd piece of ostentatious jewellery for birthdays or to say thank you or goodbye—all seemed utterly crass when he thought of giving them to Kate.

'Good.' She had turned her head away and was looking out of the window. Her voice was cold and flat.

Cristiano felt a sudden surge of anger and frustration. *Gesu*, getting into that car with the eyes of the world upon him had been one of the hardest and most frightening things he'd ever done. Everyone had been waiting to see whether he could still do it, whether he had lost his nerve. Everyone had been expecting him to fail, just as they always had.

Hell, *he* had expected it, and it had been more important to him than ever not to let it happen. It wasn't just the ghost of his mother that he had to prove himself to, it was his son.

And Kate, it seemed. He hadn't realised until now,

when she turned her head away and dismissed the achievement that had set the racing world into a tail-spin of excitement in one cool word, that he wanted to prove himself to her too.

'The sea!' Alexander's jubilant cry from the back seat broke through his thoughts. 'Look, look—there it is!'

To the right of the road the land fell away, giving an uninterrupted view over the bay. A signpost pointed to a narrow lane.

'It's down there,' Kate said.

The road that led down to a tiny village clinging to the rocks above the sea was so steep it made Courchevel look like a cricket pitch. The hedges scraped against the sides of the car and the engine throbbed as Cristiano eased it carefully round the twisting bends to a deserted car park overlooking the beach.

Released from his car seat, Alexander raced off in the direction of the path down to the sand.

'Alexander, come back! You need to put a coat on, and your wellies!' Kate shouted, but the keen wind took her voice, carrying it upwards to where the seagulls wheeled and shrieked.

'He seems to know where he's going,' Cristiano remarked dryly.

'We come here quite often.' Kate spoke in an ab-sent-minded undertone. Her eyes were fixed on the little boy, a frown of anxiety between them.

'Let's just bring his things. He's too excited to feel the cold anyway.'

'That's not the point. He shouldn't run away—there could be cars or...or he could fall, or...'

'Kate, stop.'

Reaching up, he captured her face between his hands, gently pulling it round so she had no choice but to look at him. Her eyes were shadowed with anguish, so that instead of the clear sunlit blue he remembered from Courchevel they were the same dull grey as the icy North Sea behind them. Cristiano felt a leap of something sudden and painful inside him.

Desire, yes, but he'd expected that; since Courchevel his sexual appetite had returned with a vengeance. But it was something else too. That need to protect her. To take away the worry and the pain and make her into the woman with the shy smile who had worn his shirt and brought him breakfast in bed.

To slay dragons for her.

'He's OK,' he said softly, stroking his thumbs over her cheeks. Her mouth was trembling slightly. He could feel it as his lips met hers.

It was the gentlest, most tentative of kisses—a world away from the ones they had shared before, in the Casino at Monaco and the darkness of the snowy pine forests. And yet Cristiano felt the foundations of his world shift a little. In the few brief seconds that their lips were touching it was as if he had taken a step in the dark and missed his footing...

And then she was pulling away from him, stepping

backwards, ducking her head so that her hair swung forward, hiding her face.

'Alexander. I need to find him,' she said in a choked voice, grabbing his coat and boots from the back of the car. And then she was gone.

Kate walked down the beach with rapid, furious strides, welcoming the roar of the waves in her head and the bitter sting of the wind against her cheeks.

Maybe it might bring her to her senses.

Of all the stupid, self-destructive, irresponsible things to do, kissing Cristiano in the car park had to be just about the most spectacular. Or letting him kiss her, she thought with an inward groan of misery and despair. To him, something as trivial as a kiss meant *nothing*—an image flashed into her mind of the girls she had seen at the Monaco Grand Prix four years ago, in their hotpants and bikini tops, draping themselves over the drivers—whereas to her...

To her it was oxygen to a flame that she was trying to extinguish, fuel for a fire that would consume her if she let it take hold again. He made her lose sight of reality. Of what was important. *Of Alexander.*

She would never make that mistake again.

Alexander was up ahead, running down towards the sea, occasionally wheeling back on himself to look at something on the sand or leaping over a rock. The tide was half out, and Kate's heart turned over, aching with love as she watched his slender legs pounding the hard sand, his dark hair ruffled by the wind. She should have brought a hat for him, she thought anxiously. He'd get earache, or...

'He looks pretty happy.'

Automatically she stiffened, steeling herself against the sexiness of that husky Italian drawl.

'He looks cold.'

'So do you.'

And the next thing she knew he had draped his coat over her shoulders, was taking off the whisper-soft cashmere scarf he was wearing. Hooking it around her neck, he pulled the ends of it so she was drawn closer to him, wrapping it around her. His narrow, slightly almond-shaped eyes were as warm and dark as an espresso. The heat of his body enfolded her, the scent of him filling her head.

'You're so busy looking after Alexander you forget to look after yourself.'

It was true, she realised. She had been so preoccupied with Alexander not wearing a coat that she'd forgotten to put hers on. The kiss hadn't helped her think about practicalities like that either.

She closed her eyes. Oh, God, it was so hard, this staying strong, and she was so tired. So tired of waiting for the next disaster, being on high alert for the next life-threatening danger. So tired of fighting her feelings for him all the time.

'Look, a *huge* jellyfish!'

Alexander's voice reached her distantly, over the roar of the wind and waves. Instantly her eyes snapped open. 'Don't touch it!' she called back, but Cristiano was already walking across to him, covering the sand quickly with his long strides. For a moment she watched him, mesmerised by the way the wind caught his hair and flattened his shirt against him, outlining the hard contours of the body she knew so well.

The body that had brought her such pleasure... In the pool at Monaco in the warm darkness of the Côte D'Azur night, and in the snowy silence of the Alpine chalet... Each time different, but every one so intense and exquisite that her body trembled just at her remembering...

Guiltily she jerked herself out of her mini-fantasy, and was about to follow when something stopped her. Cristiano and Alexander were both bending over the jellyfish on the sand, their faces wearing identical expressions of absorbed fascination. Cristiano had Alexander's hand in his, imperceptibly holding him back in case he should decide to try to pick it up...

And in that moment it struck her that for the first time in four years she wasn't solely responsible for her son's safety, or his happiness.

That, for now at least, she had someone to share the load.

The relief was almost overwhelming.

CHAPTER TWELVE

THE tide came in, gradually covering the expanse of flat, smooth sand on which Cristiano and Alexander played chase and looked for driftwood and flat stones to skim into the waves. In the absence of a bucket and spade to build a sandcastle they had constructed an island, hollowing out a moat around it. Cristiano had been hugely amused when Alexander suggested that they put a racetrack on it, and they had become deeply involved in planning the perfect layout of straights and corners.

Straightening up, Cristiano was surprised to see how close the sea was, and to realise that the clouds had come in, covering the sun. He smiled wryly to himself. He was someone who measured out his life, his success, in thousandths of a second, and yet he'd been so fascinated by seeing the world through this little boy's eyes that he'd completely lost track of time.

'I think it's time we went back to your *mamma*, don't you?'

They began to walk back to where Kate was sitting

in the shelter of the cliffs. He had been aware of her all the time, wrapped in his coat, her knees tucked up and her chin resting on them as she looked out to sea.

But since he'd been aware of her all the time he'd been away, he guessed that was hardly surprising. Even thousands of miles apart he'd found it impossible to stop wondering how she was, what she was doing.

At the far end of the beach a cluster of tiny grey-stone cottages huddled against the cliffs, as if cowering there from the pounding waves. Behind them the moors unfolded into the distance, a lonely expanse of green dotted with sheep and criss-crossed by uneven stone walls.

It was hardly the Amalfi coast, he thought sardonically, and yet there was something wild and beautiful about it. A quietness that caught you deep inside and made you want to come back. You could spend your life here and not get tired of watching the sea change colour and the shadows move across the hills.

His lips curved into a sudden self-mocking smile as he realised he wasn't actually thinking of the landscape at all.

Alexander stopped suddenly, tugging on Cristiano's arm as he bent to pick something up from the sand. It was a flat piece of grey rock, sharp and jagged, like slate.

'Maybe a fossil?' Alexander asked hopefully.

Cristiano turned it over in his hands, pretending to consider the possibility. 'I don't think so.'

'I take it to Mummy, just in case,' Alexander said firmly, letting go of his hand and running forward.

'Mummy! Quick, Mummy—look at this!' he shouted as he got closer.

Kate raised her head quickly, an expression of alarm on her face as she stumbled to her feet. Too late Cristiano realised that she'd been asleep. There was a red mark on her cheek where it had been resting on her knees.

'What?'

The anxiety was there again, sharpening her tone. Cristiano stepped forward, taking hold of her shoulders as she swayed slightly, holding her steady. 'It's fine. Just a stone, that's all.'

He felt her relax then, becoming pliant beneath his hands. The concern that he was increasingly feeling for her instantly flared into something far less noble.

'Maybe a fossil, Mummy,' Alexander repeated importantly. Oblivious to the sudden crackle of tension in the air, he held it out to her, his expression grave. 'You check.'

Twisting from Cristiano's grip, Kate took the stone, stumbling away from him to the rocks beneath the cliffs. Her heart was pounding, partly from the momentary panic she'd felt when she'd woken up and heard Alexander calling her like that, but mostly from Cristiano's touch. She could just about cope with it when she was prepared, when the barriers were in place, but he'd caught her off guard just then, hazy with sleep, her head still filled with the images of him playing on the sand with Alexander.

She'd watched them for a long time before she'd closed her eyes, her heart aching as she'd seen the joy on her son's face at having someone to play with him—*really* play, with the kind of carefree wholeheartedness that it seemed she was always too preoccupied to properly achieve. And seeing Cristiano—as beautiful as a sun-kissed god who had fallen to earth in the wrong place—standing with Alexander at the edge of the sea, the two of them outlined against the vastness of the ocean, had taken her breath away.

Gathering herself, she tapped the stone sharply against a rock until she felt it give a little, and then peeled it apart.

'You're right—look, there it is.'

She held it out. There on the dull grey surface was the faint but unmistakable outline of a leaf.

'Yes!' Alexander cried in triumph, running off again. 'Now I find another one!'

Left alone, Cristiano came towards her, shaking his head ruefully. He was different here, she thought with a tug of wistful longing. The diamond-hard, competitive edge that defined and drove him had softened. The icy reserve he used to keep people at a distance had melted.

'I admire him for not saying *I told you so*. I thought

there was no way he could be right. It just looked like a lump of stone to me.'

Kate dropped her gaze. 'Different' also meant harder to resist.

She had been so determined to resist him, because she'd thought she was doing the best thing for Alexander. During those interminable hours when she had sat beside him in the hospital she had promised that she would never put herself, her own interests, first again.

But suddenly everything looked very different. Suddenly it felt as if this was the best thing for Alexander. The three of them—together.

'There are lots of fossils down here.' Her voice was slightly breathless, as if she'd spent the afternoon running on the beach too. 'We find them every time we come.'

'Really?'

She nodded, pulling his coat around her. 'I bet you could find one within reach of where you're standing.'

'I never turn down a challenge.'

He bent and picked up a piece of jagged slate that was sticking up through the sand. 'OK—let's see if you're right.'

He brought it over to her. Their fingers brushed as she took it from him, and Cristiano felt the tremor that ran through her body. It shook him like an earthquake. Quickly she hit the slate on the rock, and he watched her long, clever fingers work into the seams, opening it up like a book.

'There—look.' She held it out to him, her voice a low murmur. 'It's beautiful.'

'Is there one?' he said hoarsely. 'I don't see it.'

'That's because you're not looking.'

Fixed on his, her eyes gleamed. There was a note of laughter in her voice that he hadn't heard for a long time. It sounded good. It made him feel good to know that he had put it there, for a moment chasing away the shadows and the sharpness and the fear. A slow smile spread across his face.

'I'm looking at something far more beautiful.'

They were standing in a hollow in the cliff face, sheltered from the wind and from the rest of the wide, empty beach. Impulsively, putting his hands flat against the rockface behind her, he made a prisoner of her, lowering his mouth to the angle of her jaw, sighing against the warmth of her skin.

'Cristiano, we can't…'

'Can't what?' He spoke against her neck. 'If you mean I can't strip off those incredibly sexy jeans and make love to you right here on the sand, then I'd have to agree. We are, after all, parents, and although I'm pretty new at that I have an idea that would be pushing it too far. However, if you're saying I can't do this…'

He moved his lips along to her earlobe, biting it gently, breathing out a gentle sigh that made her gasp and giggle.

'Stop. What about Alexander…?'

'It will do him the greatest good to see his mother happy for a change. Almost as much good as it'll do me to make you happy.' He pressed a line of kisses along her jaw. '*Dio*, Kate, I want you. I spent every minute, every mile of that drive from Courchevel to Yorkshire wanting you. It's all I could think of.'

Kate felt her resistance crumble, eroded away like the cliffs against her back by a force that was simply too great to withstand. With a whimpering sigh she let her head fall back, opening her mouth to him and bringing her hands up to grasp the collar of his shirt, her fists closing around it, twisting the fabric, pulling him closer as his lips worked their magic. His hands were cupping her face now, infinitely tender, warming her skin just as the strength of her longing was warming her from the inside. The noise of the wind was drowned out by the roaring of the blood in her ears, the pounding waves lost beneath the crashing of her heart as a tide of hot, slick desire swept through her.

'Mummy, I got one!'

Alexander's shout was like a bucket of cold water. Gasping, Kate pulled away just as Alexander came running around the jut of rock that had hidden them.

'I got one—look!'

Cristiano regained his composure instantly, stepping forward to take the piece of stone from him, shielding Kate with his body long enough for her to gather herself.

'*Fantastico*,' he said gravely, looking down at the small fragment of slate and tracing his fingertip over the delicate spiral imprint on its surface in a way that almost made Kate envy the long-extinct creature whose outline it was. He held it out to Alexander again. 'Well done, fossil hunter. That's the best one yet.'

'It's for you,' Alexander said easily, stretching his arms out as he attempted to balance on one leg. 'If you keep it in your pocket it will bring you good luck.'

'*Grazie.*'

Alexander toppled over, landing with a bump in the soft sand. 'What does *gratsy* mean?'

Cristiano went to sit beside him. His bare feet looked very tanned against the pale sand, but Kate noticed that they were just a couple of shades darker than Alexander's. 'It's Italian for thank you.'

Alexander looked up at him, his brown eyes filled with curiosity. 'Are you 'Talian?'

Cristiano met his gaze unflinchingly. 'Yes.'

Oh, God. Kate felt as if invisible hands were closing around her throat as she looked on, knowing that the moment she had thought about, dreamed of, wished for and dreaded for four long years was bearing down on her like a giant tidal wave. She swallowed hard, trying to steady her breathing as Alexander turned to her.

'Mummy, am *I* 'Talian?'

She met his artless chocolate-brown gaze directly. 'You're half-Italian,' she said evenly, 'and half British. Because I am British and—'

But Alexander had stopped listening. 'Yippee—I'm same as you!' he yelled, getting up in a shower of sand and throwing his arms around Cristiano's neck. 'Is it teatime soon? I'm hungry.'

Cristiano stood up in one effortless movement, Alexander clinging to him like a little monkey. Over his shoulder, Cristiano's eyes met Kate's.

'So am I,' he said softly. 'Absolutely starving.'

They stopped at a little pub on the coast road, overlooking the stretch of grey sea to Whitby Abbey in the distance. It was too early for the main crowd of evening drinkers, but the flagstoned bar was already filling up with walkers and tourists who had read about the pub's reputation for excellent food in one of the many restaurant guides. Even so, the landlord— who had seen the Campano turning into the car park and was a huge motor racing fan—showed Cristiano and Kate to the best table in the bay window, near to a glowing log fire. Alexander sat between them, his sandy legs swinging as he held a huge glass of Coca Cola in both hands.

'He'll still be bouncing off the walls at midnight if he drinks all that,' Kate said with wry softness over his head.

'*Dio*, really?' Cristiano held her gaze for a long moment, the expression on his face changing from one of amused horror to something altogether more serious and intense. Then he bent his head to Alexander's and whispered, 'Your drink looks much nicer than mine. Could I share some?'

They ordered plates of fresh lobster and a bowl of thick golden chips, taking it in turns to pass bits of succulent pink meat to Alexander. Sipping ice-cold white wine in the warmth of the fire, Kate was aware that her cheeks were flushed and glowing.

But it was nothing compared to the way she felt inside, she acknowledged with a thud of helpless desire.

With Alexander between them, she and Cristiano didn't touch at all, but she was painfully aware of his presence—the long fingers tearing into the pink flesh of the lobster, the length of his thigh on the velvet seat next to Alexander's. Every now and then their eyes met over the top of their son's head, and Kate was impaled with a longing so sharp she had to bite her lip to stop herself gasping out loud. Her mind raced ahead, counting the minutes until they could be alone.

Eventually, as Alexander was scraping the very last traces of chocolate ice-cream from his bowl, Cristiano got up to pay. Hazy with wine and warmth and need, Kate watched him walk across to the bar, ducking his head to avoid the beams, her mouth going dry as she watched him pull his wallet from the back pocket of his jeans.

'I like Cristiano,' said Alexander wistfully beside her.

'So do I,' Kate said softly, gathering him up into her arms and holding him very tightly. 'So do I.'

None of them spoke on the way home. The magic of the day hung like a fragile spell over them all.

Sitting beside Cristiano in the passenger seat, Kate felt her whole body screaming out for his touch. Unconsciously she seemed to gravitate towards him, so that as he changed gear his hand brushed her knee, making lust explode inside her like a meteor shower bright enough to light up the black moors spread out all around them. She didn't dare glance across at his perfect profile, outlined by the lights of passing cars. Already she was hanging onto control by a thread.

Alexander's head was drooping with tiredness, but he snapped back into full consciousness as Cristiano pulled up outside the house. Blinking, he looked around him.

'Home?'

'Yes, home,' Kate said, undoing her seatbelt and trying desperately to sound normal. 'And it's bedtime for you. Come on, let's get you inside and brush your teeth.'

As she leaned awkwardly into the back of the car

to undo the straps on his car seat her fingers tangled with Cristiano's, leaning in from the other side to scoop him up and carry him inside. Electricity crackled between them.

Cristiano gathered his son's small body into his arms, silently praying for the ache of his arousal to subside. *Dio*, he had never wanted a woman so much, for so long.

He'd known immediately that having a child would affect his life profoundly, in lots if different ways, but the impact on his libido wasn't something he'd anticipated, he thought with rueful amusement as he carried his small son into the house. He'd been used to having sex pretty much whenever his appetite demanded. This protracted craving was new to him, and it was as exquisite as it was excruciating.

Being near to Kate and not being able to touch her had driven him nearly to distraction. The most ordinary things seemed to take on extraordinary sensual significance—the way she'd smoothed her hair behind her ear when she was bending over to feed Alexander a morsel of lobster at dinner, the glimpse of a pale pink bra-strap against her creamy skin as she'd sat back, sipping wine, with the glow of the fire reflected in her eyes.

He wanted to peel off her clothes and examine the body that had carried his child. He wanted to cup her breasts that had fed his son in his hands and stroke them. He wanted to make her his again.

He reached the top of the stairs, ducking his head

to avoid knocking himself out. Three doors opened off the landing, but Cristiano could tell which one was Alexander's room because it had a wooden plaque in the shape of a car with a letter A on it. The house was so small that he'd have to make love to Kate very, very quietly later on…

'Not tired,' said Alexander firmly as Cristiano pushed open the bedroom door with his shoulder. 'Want a story. Want Cristiano to read me a story.'

Maledizione o ostia.

He hadn't even seen it coming. Carefully keeping his expression blank, he put his son down on the bed and switched on the lamp. Soft light illuminated a small room in which everything from the bedlinen to the frieze painted around the top of the walls was a homage to cars.

Kate appeared in the doorway behind him. Her voice was hushed and soothing.

'Come on, sweetheart. Pyjamas, then teeth.'

Diving under the pillow, Alexander pulled out a pair of soft blue pyjamas, unsurprisingly featuring a picture of a racing car on the front. Tucking them under his arm, he raced out of the room.

Left alone, Cristiano stood in the centre of the room. His heart was thudding and the palms of his hands were suddenly slick with sweat. A tall bookcase stood behind the door, crammed full with books—serious-looking ones, with gold-embossed spines, mixed in with millions of slim, brightly coloured ones.

He should have anticipated this. How could he have been so stupid?

That was easy, he thought with an inward laugh of bitter despair. Hadn't he always been stupid? For the last twenty years he'd put everything he had into running away, trying desperately to prove that he was something other than the worthless failure he had been labelled by the teachers at school and by his disappointed mother. But this tiny room, with the frayed carpet and the line of toy cars on the window-sill, was where his demons had caught up with him at last. Where he finally had to admit that there was nowhere left to run.

Alexander came in again. He was wearing his pyjamas and his face was scrubbed clean of chocolate ice cream. As he climbed into bed he looked unbearably small and sweet. Looking down, Cristiano could see the hollow at the nape of his fragile neck, the bumps of his spine. His heart felt as if it was splitting open.

His child.

His son.

Alexander looked up at him with liquid brown eyes that were full of trust. 'Please can you read me a story?'

'I—'

The words dried up in his mouth. Cristiano thrust his hand through his hair. He felt slightly faint.

'No story tonight.' Kate's voice was firm as she crossed the room, bending swiftly to turn out the light and give Alexander a kiss. 'It's late, and you're tired, but if you lie down I'm sure Cristiano will talk to you for a little while about the racing cars he drives.'

'*Si*. Of course.'

As Kate walked past him to leave the room she glanced up at him. In the half-light from the landing his face bore an expression that was somewhere between relief and despair.

'I love you, Cristiano.'

'I love you too. *Ti amo, piccolino.*'

Pulling the door shut gently behind him, Cristiano stood out on the landing. Leaning against the wall, he exhaled heavily, despair weighing on him like a curse.

I love you.

He had never said those words before. He wasn't even sure that he had felt them before—not in the fierce, primitive way he had felt them just now, when he had bent to kiss his son's cheek. The impact of what it meant to be a father had hit him with the force of an avalanche, and he knew that he would do anything—*anything*—for his child.

If he could.

But what about the things he couldn't do? What about those? Could he really be a good father? Or was it just another thing that he was destined to fail at? Was he going to let his son down in the same way as his mother?

He had got away with it tonight, thanks to Kate's

lucky intervention. But how long could he hide it? How long could he go on fooling her that he was something he wasn't?

A shaft of light fell across the dark landing, and suddenly a shadow moved across it. He watched her move, watched the outline of her body perform its silent shadow-dance across the floor, and his spiralling thoughts stilled.

Arousal hardened him, temporarily blotting out the bitterness and the doubts.

A floorboard creaked as he moved across the floor, and the shadow twisted and undulated as she came to the door. And then he forgot about the flat monochrome outline of her because she was there in front of him, the lamplight turning her skin to warm honey and her hair to molten gold.

'All right?'

Wordlessly he nodded, a lump in his throat. Suddenly he wanted to tell her—wanted to spill it all out and lay himself bare before her.

'Cristiano...I—' Her voice vibrated with an emotion he couldn't quite identify, but which seemed to reach down and touch him inside like ethereal fingers. In his state of heightened, painful arousal it was almost more than he could bear.

And he knew that at that moment he didn't want to talk. Didn't want to think. He just wanted to lose himself in her sweetness. Crossing the landing in one stride, he pulled her into his arms, pushing the door shut as he pressed his mouth down on hers. Her body was warm, her mouth as eager as his. With hungry, hurried fingers she pulled his shirt free of his trousers, sliding her hands up his chest, moaning her pleasure against him.

Swiftly he undid the button of her jeans, pulling them downwards along with her underwear as they both fell back onto the bed. The springs gave a screech of protest that made both of them freeze for a moment, clinging together as they listened for sounds from outside.

None came. But the interruption had altered the tempo of their passion. For long moments they gazed at each other before their lips slowly met again, hesitantly exploring, tasting, caressing. Rising above her, Cristiano unhurriedly trailed the tip of his tongue down the sweep of her throat. Her skin tasted faintly of the sea. She let her head fall back and he could hear her uneven breathing as he reached the neck of her T-shirt.

Gently he took hold of the hem, bringing it up over her head, his head reeling as her beautiful body was revealed. Her breasts were spilling out of the pink bra, so he slid his arms around her, pulling her against him as he unhooked it.

He had to clamp his teeth together to stop himself shouting out as he felt her warm, lovely flesh against his chest. Trailing his fingertips across her back, he lowered his head so that his lips hovered over one rose-tipped breast.

Time stalled.

Dio…Mio Dio… She was so beautiful. So incredibly beautiful. Opening his mouth, he let out a deep, shuddering sigh, watching her flesh tighten and harden as his breath caressed it. His whole body burned with the need to sink inside her, but he held back, forcing himself to take it slowly as he covered her breast in whisper-soft butterfly kisses, gradually moving his lips inwards towards her nipple.

She gave a whimpering gasp, raising her hands to cover her mouth. Cristiano felt wild, visceral satisfaction surge though him as her body tensed with pleasure. Her pleasure, her happiness, were the only things in the world that mattered.

But then she was gripping his shoulders, pulling him away. He raised his head, his head swimming with lust.

'Kate?'

'I want to see you,' she breathed brokenly. 'I want to feel your body against me and I want to look into your eyes.'

Very slowly she began to undo the buttons of his shirt, her gaze never faltering, her eyes gleaming like sapphires in the lamplight, seeming to look right down into his soul. It took every ounce of the self-control it had taken Cristiano a lifetime to acquire to keep still, to keep silent as her hands moved down to the fastening of his jeans.

Her breath quickened as she undid them. Her lips parted and for a brief second her eyelids fluttered.

It was enough. Almost delirious with need, he

kicked off his jeans and hitched her further up on the bed, rising above her as she opened herself up for him.

Biting the insides of his cheeks he entered her very slowly, watching her face, noticing how her eyes never left his. They were locked together. Lost together. Her hands were on his shoulders, and then, as the rhythm of their bodies grew faster, she let him go, throwing them wide on the pillows, her fingers curling and uncurling as waves of pleasure rocked her.

He sensed her tensing, arching, and felt his own body gather itself in response. Then she brought her hand to her mouth, covering it as her hips ground against him and her internal muscles tightened convulsively on him.

For a moment he stilled completely as her high, breathless gasp quivered in the silence, then he gathered her to him, holding her tight against his chest as he shattered inside her.

Kate lay very still, listening to the beat of her own heart, the distant sound of the traffic on the main road that bypassed the village. Ordinary sounds, the sounds she had heard almost every night for the last three years, since she had moved here with a newborn Alexander.

This was the floor she had paced with him during those sleepless nights when he had been fretful and colicky, when she had stood at the window rocking him and staring out into the darkness, watching the lights of the cars. Counting them. Wishing and praying that one set of them would belong to Cristiano's car as he came to find her.

He was here now. And in that moment nothing else mattered.

CHAPTER THIRTEEN

IT WAS still dark outside as Cristiano eased himself from the warmth of the old brass bed. The floorboards were icy beneath his feet.

Dio, he must sort out something formal with Kate about money, he thought grimly, picking up his clothes from the floor and making his way as quietly as possible across the creaking landing. Just in time he remembered to duck his head as he went into the miniature bathroom. This house seemed to have been built for dolls, or for families of Victorian Yorkshire miners, so used to crawling along claustrophobic tunnels that they would have had no problem walking around with a permanent stoop at home.

Unlike him. If they were going to be a proper family they would need a proper family home to live in. More than one, probably. He imagined that Kate would want to keep a base here, near her family and friends, but it was important for him to have somewhere in Europe, to be close to the best facilities for training. It didn't have to be Monaco, he thought vaguely as he splashed water on his face. Monza was good...

Straightening up, he looked at his reflection in the mirror above the basin. *It's over,* he thought hoarsely. *The years of running away are over. I've found someone I want to stay with.*

There was just the small matter of telling her about his past, he reflected soberly as he pulled on his clothes. He paused, feeling panic grip him for a second at the thought of what she might say. Would she despise him for his lack of academic ability? Would she be able to spend her life with someone who wasn't her intellectual equal and who had spent his teenage years bunking off school and stealing cars?

He clenched his fists, pressing them against his throbbing temples for a moment, closing his eyes as he struggled to regain his grip on rationality.

It was the first Grand Prix of the season in just over a week. If he could get back out there and prove himself, maybe he would be worthy of her. Maybe then she would see him as someone she could spend her life with.

The thin light of dawn was stealing through the curtains as he went softly back into the bedroom. His leather holdall lay on the floor by the window and he unzipped it, wincing slightly at the noise, and took something out of the inside pocket.

'Cristiano?'

Her voice was soft and throaty. Tensing himself

against another onslaught of desire, he turned to look at her.

'*Si?*'

'You're dressed.' As she struggled to sit up he saw the look of bewilderment on her face.

'I have to go.'

She lifted one slender arm to her head, frowning as she pushed her tumbled hair back from her face. 'Where?'

Cristiano felt desire stab him in the guts again, and steeled himself against it. If he gave in to the temptation to have her again now, there was a very real danger that he'd never leave.

'Bahrain,' he said with an apologetic smile.

'Oh.' It was a little indrawn breath, as if she had just got a paper cut.

'It's OK,' Cristiano said gruffly, going towards her and putting the envelope Suki had organised for him down on top of a pile of thick novels on the bedside table.

'What's that?' Her eyes were huge and frightened as she looked at the envelope.

'Tickets. For you and Alexander—flights and a hotel and the Grand Prix itself. He'll adore—'

'No.' Her face was suddenly ashen, her expression closed and blank. Clutching the bedcovers across her breasts, she reached for the washed out silk kimono that hung from a hook on the back of the door. 'Sorry, Cristiano. I can't.'

For a moment he thought it was something to do

with the money, and that he'd offended her prickly
sense of pride by making a gesture that she considered too extravagant. 'Don't be silly, Kate. It's
nothing—'

She'd got out of bed. His voice faltered as she
turned away from him and he caught a glimpse of
her pale, slender back and the curve of her perfect
behind just before it was covered by faded rose-pink
silk.

'You don't understand.' She was trying to keep
her voice quiet, so she didn't wake Alexander, but
he could hear the edge of hysteria in it. 'I can't go. I
can't watch you do that again. And I don't want my
son watching either.'

With that, she walked out of the room in a rustle
of pink silk, leaving Cristiano standing by the bed.
A slow beat of anger started up inside him. Cursing
softly in Italian, he gathered up his bag and swung
it over his shoulder as he followed her down the
stairs.

He found her in the tiny kitchen. Her back was to
him and she was filling the kettle at the sink.

'He's my son too.'

His voice was dangerously quiet. Kate turned.
Standing in the doorway, he looked impossibly huge
and intimidating. And distant. Very, very distant.

'Then you shouldn't want to encourage him,' she
whispered.

'Encourage him? In what way, exactly?'

'To do what you do. To think it's a good idea to put his life on the line for public entertainment.'

Cristiano's eyes glittered like black diamonds. The bliss they'd shared only a few hours ago, the intimacy, was like a fragment of a delicious dream, fading into oblivion with the gathering light. Kate's head spun. She felt as if she had stepped into a lift, only to find it was on some other floor and she was plunging down a dark, empty shaft.

'That's what you think I do?'

'That *is* what you do, Cristiano. I watched you, re-member?' Kate's voice was harder now, firmer, as she busied herself with the familiar, mindless routine of making coffee. 'I watched women draping themselves all over you, and film crews and journalists swarming around, and crowds all screaming your name. And then I watched your car smash into a barrier and burst into flame—' She broke off, giving a bitter parody of a laugh. 'There's nothing clever about killing yourself in a car, you know—any amateur can do that. Like my brother. Like my father.'

And that was it. It was the old nightmare from her childhood, back to get her after all these years. She had lowered her guard—just as she had in Courchevel—and this was what happened.

Leaning against the doorframe, Cristiano tipped his head back, looking at her through narrowed eyes. 'I never claimed to be doing something clever,' he drawled softly. 'I'm just doing what I can to—'

'What?' Adrenaline pulsed through her as she cut

him off. 'Show the world that you're not a failure? The fact is Cristiano, no one but you thinks that. You might have had a hard time at school, but to everyone else you're a god—and to Alexander more than anyone.'

It was as if she'd slapped him. Suddenly the languor was gone and he was standing bolt upright, rigid, his hands clenched into fists as he came towards her.

'What did you say?'

Her chin rose an inch. 'I said your son needs you.'

'Before that.' His lips barely moved as he spoke. 'About school. How did you know about that?'

'Because you told me.' The words came out with quiet emphasis. 'You told me everything on that first night we spent together. You told me about the struggle you had at school, and about the sacrifices your mother made to give you an education. You told me about how disappointed she was when you didn't do well, when you started skipping lessons and hanging out with a bad crowd. You told me about how Silvio came to your rescue when you stole his car, offering you an apprenticeship instead of pressing charges, and you told me how angry she was when you accepted it.'

'*Enough.*'

The word was like the lash of a whip on Kate's tightly reined emotions. For a while yesterday it had seemed so possible because it had felt so *right*—the three of them together. But now she knew that she had been fooling herself. There could be no happy ending because she had fallen in love with a man who represented everything that scared her most.

'I know how she felt, Cristiano. She loved you. She just wanted you to be safe.'

'No,' he spat, his eyes burning in a face that was suddenly parchment-pale. 'You're wrong about that. She *didn't* love me. She hated me. I made her life an utter misery, and then I killed her.'

There was a small, stunned silence.

Turning away, Cristiano dragged a hand over his eyes. Suddenly he looked unbearably weary. 'See—I didn't quite tell you *everything*, did I?'

'That's not true,' Kate whispered, in a voice that sounded as if she had just swallowed strychnine.

'Yes, it is. She had cancer. She didn't tell me. Who knows? She might have tried, but I was never there— sometimes I didn't come home for days. She must have known that she had it for ages, but she didn't go to the doctor because all her money was taken up with paying for my education. And because she knew that if she went into hospital I'd go completely off the rails.'

'But that shows that she was thinking of you.' Kate was pleading the case of a woman she'd never met. 'Putting you first.'

'She wanted me to *better* myself.' His voice dripped irony. Pulling out a chair, he sprawled into it, propping his elbows on the table, raking his hands through his hair. 'To pull myself out of the poverty my waster of a father had left her in. To her, that meant getting a good education and being a doctor or a lawyer. When I started my apprenticeship with Campano she thought I had signed up for a life of dead-end manual labour. It was like throwing everything she'd ever given me back in her face.'

The coffee stood cooling in mugs on the table. Neither of them picked one up. Kate's head throbbed as she struggled to find the right words. It felt like picking her way through a shark-infested swamp.

'That's why it mattered to you to win, I know,' she said hoarsely. 'To prove to her that you were a success. But that's over now. You don't have anything to prove to anyone.'

'Yes, I do. To my son.'

There was something terrifyingly final about the way he said it. Looking up at him, Kate knew with a chilling despair that the sharks were circling, closing in on her.

'He'll love you anyway—no matter what you do,' she said, unable to keep the desperation from ringing through every syllable. 'That's the thing about being a father: to your child you're always a god, and it doesn't matter if you're a bus driver or a racing driver.'

Leaning back in his chair, he smiled, but his eyes were flinty. 'Exactly. That's why I have to do something to deserve that respect—or else one day he'll find out that I'm nothing.'

'You're not nothing.' Kate suddenly realised she

was very cold. Speaking through clenched teeth, she pulled her robe more tightly around her. 'You're dyslexic, Cristiano. You have a really common condition that makes reading and writing and letter recognition difficult. It's not usually fatal, but in your case it just might be—because it's combined with an arrogant pride that means you have to prove yourself all the time.'

He got to his feet, looking at her with hollow eyes. 'You knew about this all along?'

'Yes.' It was a breathless whisper. She could feel the tears burning at the back of her eyes, the sobs swelling in her throat. 'I knew because once you trusted me enough to tell me. You felt enough to want to explain. When I came to find you again, I hoped that you might still feel the same way—' She broke off and gave an odd, hiccupping gasp. 'And then I found out that the crash had made you forget. And I *so* wanted you to feel that way all over again. But you didn't.'

He was utterly still, as if he had been turned to stone. The expression on his face was one of tightly restrained pain. Raising his hands, he held them up for a moment, and then let them fall to his sides again.

'I asked you to marry me once before, and you said no,' he said, in a voice like barbed wire. 'Well, I'm asking again now. Marry me, Kate—not for Alexander's sake, or to give him a stable background, but for yours. For ours. Because I—'

'No, Cristiano!' The words came out on a great tearing sob. 'I can't spend the rest of my life waiting to lose you! I can't sit on the sidelines, or in the pit lane, or at home, and watch you kill yourself. I can't live off the money you earn from gambling with your life.'

He backed off, his hands curling into fists now, his expression hardening so that his perfect face might have been sculpted from marble. 'So you'd rather not be happy, because then that happiness can't be taken away from you?'

Kate made herself look at him—even though it hurt, even though her whole face felt numb, as if she was standing in the teeth of a raging, icy gale. Slowly she shook her head.

'I wouldn't be happy.'

It was a whisper. Like a confession. Hearing it, Cristiano closed his eyes for the briefest moment before his face became expressionless again.

'In that case I won't ask you again,' he said harshly. 'I'll get my solicitor to be in touch about Alexander. I hope we can sort it out amicably.'

And then he turned and went, and Kate was left standing dry-eyed and shaking in the kitchen. She didn't move at all as she listened to the throb of the car's engine grow fainter in the distance, until the silence swallowed it up and she was alone.

CHAPTER FOURTEEN

KATE went back to work.

There didn't seem to be anything else to do. It was part of picking up the pieces. Getting on with life. Dominic had been brilliant about giving her as much time off as she needed while Alexander was recovering, but following his energetic display on the beach with Cristiano she could hardly fool herself that he needed her constant attention any more. Besides, he was probably better off with her mother at the moment—or any random stranger who would be able to hold a conversation with him without snapping his head off or bursting into tears mid-sentence.

Even on a sunny March day the Clearspring office was gloomy. Kate sat at her desk, miserably aware of people's curious stares and the fact that the entire office seemed to suddenly have a reason to walk past her desk. Word had clearly got out that Kate Edwards, the mousy copywriter, was actually the secret mistress of racing legend Cristiano Maresca and mother of his love-child.

Sooner or later she would have to disabuse them of the first notion.

In the kitchen the Campano calendar had been replaced by one from the Healthy Schools account, featuring Alice Apple and Percy Pear. Waiting for the kettle to boil, Kate picked up a newspaper someone had left on top of the microwave, letting her eyes move dully over the headlines without really taking them in.

She had totally lost touch with what was going on in the world, she realised with a stab of guilty misery. In the shiny side of the kettle her gaunt face stared back at her, the surface curve distorting her reflection so her red-rimmed eyes looked huge and the dark circles around them even bigger. Impatiently she turned her attention back to the paper, intending to check out her horoscope and the television listings for tonight, when a photograph on the back caught her eye.

At first she thought her mind was playing tricks on her, imprinting the face she longed to see onto every dark-haired man her eyes fell on. And then the headline above the picture filtered into her numb brain.

MARESCA'S ERRATIC PERFORMANCE CAUSE FOR CAMPANO CONCERN.

Her heart stopped, then started up again with a jolt that felt as if crash pads had just been pressed to her chest. Her mouth was dry, her hands shaking so much it was difficult to hold the paper still enough to read.

Cristiano Maresca's much anticipated return this season looks like it could be causing one or two headaches for the Campano Team. The thirty-two-year-old Italian, who suffered massive head injuries in a crash at Monaco four years ago, has been reported to have performed 'erratically' in pre-race time trials this week, after missing two days entirely.

'Cristiano is well aware of the demands of the forthcoming season, and has taken some time out before it begins to resolve some personal issues,' said Suki Conti of Campano. 'When he takes his place on the grid this weekend it will be with one hundred per cent focus and commitment.'

'Ah. There you are.'

Kate looked up with a little gasp. Dominic was leaning around the doorway, his face lined with concern. 'I've just been to your office to find you.'

Kate attempted a kind of laugh. It came out as a sob.

'I came to hide from the onlookers. You know, I'd heard that there were people who stop to look at c-car accidents, but until today I never really thought it was true.'

As she'd said the bit about car accidents her voice had cracked, and suddenly Dominic had crossed the room to her and was putting his arms around her rigid shoulders. Taking the newspaper from her, he glanced down at the page she'd been reading.

He sighed, looking at her with an expression of infinite compassion.

'Something tells me you're not quite ready for all this yet. Look, why don't you take the rest of the week off? The Healthy Schools account is all up to date at the moment, so there's not much for you to do here.'

Kate was just about to argue that she was fine, when it dawned on her that he was saying she was more of a hindrance than a help in the office right now.

In a daze, she drove to her mother's. Margaret Edwards came to the door, wiping her hands on an apron, a familiar expression of alarm crossing her face when she saw Kate.

A shaft of sadness pierced Kate's numbness. Grief had dominated her mother's life for twenty years. Having lost both her husband and her son in road accidents, there was a part of her that expected every knock at the door to be a kindly female police officer bringing bad news.

'What is it, love?' she said worriedly, standing aside to let Kate in. 'Alexander's having his afternoon nap upstairs—I wasn't expecting you until five, as usual. Has something happened?'

Kate took a ragged breath, leaning against the familiar faded wallpaper of the hallway for a moment.

'No… Yes… *Oh, Mum…*'

And then she was in her mother's arms, and the racking sobs she had been holding back since Cristiano had walked away from her were gripping her, the tears that she had been too numb to cry pouring down her face and soaking into Margaret's cotton cardigan.

'Kate, love?'

'I'm in here.'

The door opened and Margaret appeared, carrying two floral china mugs of strong brown tea. She set them down on the bedside table. Will's bedside table.

Sitting on the bed, Kate moved up a little to make room for her mother. After the storm of weeping she had come upstairs to wash her face and check on Alexander, and for the first time in years had found herself opening the door to Will's old room.

'Do you mind me coming in here?' she asked quietly now, picking up a mug and blowing on the steaming surface.

Pulling her cardigan across her thin chest with red, work-roughened hands, Margaret looked around. Everything was exactly as it had been on the evening that Will had left it, dressed in his new jeans for a night out with friends. His black towelling robe still hung on the back of the door, the bed was still made, the posters of his favourite models and pop stars and sports heroes still lined the walls—some of them looking a little dated now.

Except Cristiano. He looked younger and more wicked, but just as gorgeous.

'No, love, I don't mind. I often come in here myself—to dust and that—but just because it makes me feel better as well. Closer to him, I suppose.'

The tears had left Kate feeling scoured out and oddly calm, as if she could think about things more clearly now. 'How did you manage after Dad died?' she asked.

'There's many would say I didn't manage at all.' Picking up her tea, Margaret absent-mindedly wiped away the wet ring left by the mug with a tissue. 'The doctor gave me pills, and they did help take the edge off the guilt, and people were very kind...'

Kate frowned. 'Guilt? Why guilt? Dad was killed in an accident on the way to work.'

Margaret took a sip of tea and put her mug down carefully. 'We'd had an argument that morning before he left. Something daft that blew up over nothing, but it haunted me for years.' She gave Kate a watery smile. 'Still does, if I'm honest. I couldn't get the idea out of my head that I'd caused the accident by distracting him, so his mind wasn't on the road.'

'It was the other driver's fault, Mum,' Kate said gently. 'They said so at the inquest, didn't they?'

Margaret shrugged her thin shoulders in the

washed-out blouse and threadbare cardigan, her fingers twisting her gold wedding band. 'That made no difference to me. To me it's always felt like my fault, and even if it wasn't—'

She broke off, staring down at her hands for a moment. 'Even if it wasn't,' she continued quietly, 'I still can't forgive myself for not telling him that I loved him that day. It's only after someone's gone that you realise what a rare and precious thing it is—love.' She shook her head dismissively. 'Everything else is just details.'

'Oh, Mum…'

Kate sighed. While Margaret had been talking she had got to her feet had gone to stand in front of the picture of Cristiano. His dark eyes stared out at her, narrowed, inscrutable, and looking into them, listening to her mother's voice—so wistful and full of regret—suddenly she found everything seemed very clear.

Turning round, she said, 'Mum, could you possibly have Alexander for me this weekend?'

Margaret blinked, taken aback but clearly pleased at the question. 'Yes love, you know I always love having him. But why?'

'I think…I'm going to Bahrain.'

Cristiano kept his gaze fixed on the pair of perfectly painted lips an inch from his.

He was very still, gritting his teeth as Francine Fournier shone the light into first one eye and then the other. He could feel her breath feathering the bare skin of his chest, and when he breathed in his head was filled with her perfume, and while it was all so different from Kate's, it still reminded him of her.

Like everything else.

'OK, you can get dressed now, Cristiano.'

Clicking off the miniature torch, Francine straightened up, her silk-lined skirt rustling as she went to sit down at the desk.

'It's all looking great,' she said neutrally, beginning to scribble rapid notes in a file. 'And in view of the fact that you haven't had any recurrence of the problems you were having previously, I'm perfectly happy to pass you fit to drive today.'

'*Buono.*'

Cristiano reached for his T-shirt and pulled it over his head, getting down from the couch. Francine looked up at him pointedly for a second, her pen hovering over the page.

'I assume that that *is* good news?' she enquired dryly.

'Of course.' Cristiano managed a sort of smile as he went towards the door. 'Sorry. I'm just a little tense. I'll be fine when I get out there.'

That was what he hoped, anyway. Driving— winning—was the way he'd always obliterated his problems. There was no time to think about anything but survival when you were hurtling along a track at two hundred miles an hour. No time to think about the fact that you couldn't make the mother of your child happy. The only thing was, he wasn't sure that the forty nine laps of the race would be long enough for him.

'Just one more thing before you go,' Francine said, taking a sheet of paper from her folder and studying it. 'I know this has no bearing on your race fitness, but I thought you might like to know. I checked over the tests you did the other day—for dyslexia.'

Cristiano didn't allow the merest flicker of emotion to pass across his face.

'And?'

Francine frowned. 'It appears that you're quite severely dyslexic—to such an extent that I would certainly expect it to have been picked up at school. Was it never mentioned to you or your parents?'

'Not as a medical condition,' Cristiano said acidly. 'My astonishing stupidity was mentioned often—to me, my mother, and the rest of the school.'

Francine nodded slowly. 'Thankfully ignorance like that is pretty rare these days, but I'm sorry that you had to endure it. It can't have been easy.'

'No.'

So Kate was right. Straight away she had understood the problem that had confounded him his whole life. She had shone a clear, pure light into a darkness that he had thought impenetrable.

Francine watched him as he got to his feet and went to the door. Her sensible, scientific, happily married heart gave a little flutter. Indigestion, she told herself firmly.

'Good luck for the race today.'

'*Grazie.*'

'Oh—and Cristiano? Thank you for the champagne. There was absolutely no need for you to do that. The chalet is empty far too much—it was my pleasure to let you use it.'

He turned to her with a smile that was as beautiful as it was poignant.

'I can assure you, the pleasure was all mine.'

It was all a question of perspective, Kate observed numbly as she looked out of the plane window and down onto the desert below. A few years ago—hell, a few weeks ago—the thought of a seven-hour flight would have reduced her to a quivering mass of panic.

Now it barely even aroused a flicker of concern. In spite of electrical problems that had meant an extended stopover in Amsterdam, the vague potential for mid-air collisions and engine failure was nothing compared to the very real horror she felt at living the rest of her life without Cristiano.

'Ladies and gentlemen, following our delayed departure from Amsterdam we will shortly be landing at Bahrain International Airport.' The captain's voice over the speakers was indolent to the point of boredom. 'If you look out of your window now you'll see the Bahrain International Circuit, where the Grand Prix is due to start approximately forty minutes from now. The weather in Bahrain is a pleasant twenty-two degrees at the moment, with a light breeze...'

A ripple of interest ran through the plane and everyone craned to look below. The scene reminded Kate of Alexander's toy racetrack—a strip of grey, winding in a series of improbably sharp turns through a landscape of arid sand. Sunlight glittered off metal, flags rippled in the warm air, and people moved around in an undulating mass, like a breeze across a field of multi-coloured grasses.

She felt sick.

Forty minutes to go. *Please let me get there in time*, she prayed.

If anything, it was the absence of nerves that worried him. All around he could see the other drivers, receiving last-minute instructions from team bosses and engineers, giving interviews, hopping from foot to foot with barely restrained energy and aggression, like boxers about to go into the ring.

Cristiano felt removed from all the frenzy and excitement. Tucked inside his overalls, right next to his heart, was the fossil Alexander had given him, and as he walked from the garages into the media circus on the grid he put his hand up to touch the hardness of it. It was madness, carrying it on him like that—if his car caught fire and he was stuck inside the wreck it would absorb the furnace-like heat instantly, burning through his skin.

The Campano team were clustered around the car,

their emerald-green colours standing out vividly like an oasis. The desert lay all around…an endless vista of sand which reminded him painfully of Alexander, running across the beach in Yorkshire…

Dio. He needed to focus.

Suki turned round, her catlike eyes lighting up as she saw him, and in that moment he felt something shift again inside his head. She came forward, reaching up to kiss his cheek…

Where was Kate?

The question appeared in his head from nowhere, and he felt a sensation like a small electric shock in his brain. He pulled away from Suki, looking around, suddenly filled with an inexplicable conviction that Kate was here—that she was looking for him too.

Around the other side of the car, Silvio was talking to a cluster of reporters who were all pointing their microphones at him like tribesmen wielding spears. Cristiano's heart was pounding. Without thinking he turned and headed back in the direction of the garages, ignoring the TV reporters who held microphones out to him and shouted questions as he passed. Desperately he raked the crowd with his eyes. Kate was here. He was certain of it. He broke into a run, feeling the sweat start to pool in the small of his back, knowing he should be conserving his hydration levels for later in the race, but somehow not managing to translate that abstract knowledge into physical reality.

He was breathing hard as he reached the garages. He stopped, looking around, expecting to see her.

She had to be there.

She had to... He was so sure...

Raking his sweat-damp hair back from his forehead, he spun round, speaking softly under his breath.

'Please... Please...'

'Cristiano!'

It was Suki's voice behind him. She was running over, her hair bouncing over her shoulders like some clichéd shampoo advert. 'Come on—it's time to go!'

Despair knifed him between his ribs. He cast one more look around, then with a low, ragged curse began to walk back to his car.

The roads were wide and fringed with palm trees. The desert stretched out on all sides, flat and beige and unfinished-looking, contrasting with the clean perfection of the streets and buildings.

'How long will it take to get there?' Kate asked from between clenched teeth.

In the rearview mirror the taxi driver's currant-like eyes were sharp with curiosity.

'Not long. I drive fast—like the racing drivers.' The eyes crinkled with amusement. 'Don't worry. I get you there for start of the race.'

Kate stifled a moan of frustration, staring out of the window at the pristine buildings. 'That's too late.

There's something I have to say to someone before the race.'

'OK.' He glanced at her uncertainly, as if she was mentally unstable and potentially dangerous. 'Nearly there now. Which stand are you in?'

Kate looked down at the laminated pass Cristiano had left for her and read out the information. The eyes in the mirror widened.

'VIP area,' the taxi driver said in a tone of renewed respect. 'Don't worry—nearly there now.'

A bright red banner stretched above the road, welcoming visitors to the Bahrain International Circuit. Kate's blood throbbed painfully through her veins as if it had been thickened with treacle. Through the front windscreen she could see an impressive round tower, rising up over the rest of the stands and buildings, dominating the landscape. As they came to a gate manned by security guards the taxi driver slowed, and she handed over her pass for scanning.

Impassively the guard looked at it, then handed it back and waved the car through. The pointed tops of the stands loomed larger, as pale and delicate as tented canopies from some *Arabian Nights* fantasy. Kate was sitting on the edge of her seat, every atom of her being willing the car onward.

'You are big motor racing fan?' the driver asked.

Kate gave a choked laugh. 'I hate it.'

The eyes in the rearview mirror blinked in surprise. The English lady with a face as white as her T-shirt clearly *was* mad.

'Then may I ask why you come here?'

Kate exhaled a shaky breath. 'Because I suddenly realised that love is a million times stronger than that.'

The dark eyes softened as the car came to a standstill at another set of gates. 'I leave you here, miss.'

Her hands were shaking as she reached into her bag for money and got out of the car. Her legs nearly gave way beneath her.

'Good luck,' the taxi driver called after her.

She handed her pass to another set of security guards, who frowned down at it for a second, then back up at her.

'A guest of Cristiano Maresca?'

'Where do I have to go?' she gasped. 'I need to find him before the race starts.'

'Through there. But you'll have to hurry—'

At that moment the ground beneath them began to shake with what felt like the beginnings of an earthquake. A high-pitched hum vibrated in the air, suddenly rising like a siren to an ear-splitting scream.

'Ah…' said the guard apologetically. 'Sorry. Too late.'

The sun was low on the track, shining through a haze of fuel. A white plume of smoke rose up from the Ferrari in front of Cristiano as they came into the second corner, making it impossible to see.

Cristiano kept going, his lungs bursting as the acceleration pressed back on him. He was driving blind, with only his split-second reflexes between him and oblivion. And Alexander's fossil, he thought with a sudden burst of elation as the choking cloud lifted. Another corner. On Cristiano's nearside wing a car spun out of control, spiralling away behind him. Cristiano felt his elation die a little as he let out a vicious curse.

Silvio's voice on the team radio was reassuring. 'It's OK, Cristiano. Plenty of room at the front now. Move in. Show them that you're back.'

You don't have to prove anything to anyone...

Swearing softly again, Cristiano hit the brakes. This wasn't meant to happen, he thought grimly. The noise of the engine and the pressure of the G-force and the sheer bloody need to stay alive should make it impossible to hear Kate's voice inside his head. That was why he did this—to escape the tangled mess of complicated emotions over which he had no control.

To forget.

But he couldn't. And in that moment he felt another flashbulb sensation as the track in front of him disappeared and he *remembered...*

He remembered last time. Monaco. Going back to look for Kate before he got in the car. That was why he'd thought she was here today, he realised, as a clear picture of her in a blue T-shirt—*his* blue T-shirt?—appeared in his head.

And she had turned and smiled at him, and he had pulled her into the garages and kissed her and laughed because she had told him to drive carefully.

A shower of sparks flew up from the brakes of the car in front. Swerving out of his wake, Cristiano found some clear space on the outside of the bend.

'Move in, move in!' Silvio yelled over the radio. 'You're losing seconds!'

And suddenly it all made perfect sense. All this time he had surrounded himself with people who urged him on, wanting a piece of him, wanting him to reach higher, drive faster. And all he'd ever really wanted was someone who loved him enough to tell him to stop.

His mother had wanted that. And so did Kate.

He slowed down. Silvio was shouting so loudly in his headset that his voice was an incoherent crackle of noise. The pit lane entrance loomed in front of him and he swung in. The pit crew sprang forward, looking alarmed. Silvio appeared from behind them, pushing his way to the front, mouthing apoplectically as Cristiano brought the throbbing, shaking car to a standstill.

Yanking off his steering wheel, he levered himself up out of the car. He was fleetingly aware of cameras closing in, but then something else caught his eye, making his head snap round as forcefully as if he'd just taken a corner at one hundred and eighty miles an hour.

Kate.

It was Kate.

She was standing behind Silvio, both hands pressed to her mouth in a way that in that single, incredulous, sunlit moment made him think of when they'd made love in her brass bed in Yorkshire and she'd had to stop herself crying out.

'What the hell are you *doing*?' Silvio yelled, his face almost purple with rage. 'The track was wide open in front of you. The car was going like a dream—'

'I know.'

Cristiano pulled off his head support and his helmet, tossing them back into the cockpit of the car. His eyes never left Kate. He wanted to tear open his overalls and pull his beating heart from his chest, offering it to her on the palm of his hand.

'You know? You *know*? *Per Madre di Dio*, Cristiano, the race could have been *yours*...'

'I know,' he said again, moving past Silvio and going towards her. 'But the thing is, I just realised I don't want it.'

The huge desert sun brushed her hair with gold-dust and turned the tears that welled in her eyes into shimmering pools of molten gold.

'Don't say that—please,' she croaked hoarsely, and for a moment his heart stopped as icy fear gripped him. Real fear.

'Kate—'

'No. Let me finish.' She reached up and pressed her finger to his lips, hushing him. Her throat felt as if she'd swallowed an entire desert of sand. 'I came here to tell you—'

But the other cars, still grouped together, were coming around the circuit again, the ever-present scream of their engines rising to an ear-splitting shriek. She kept her eyes fixed on his, desperate to make herself heard above the noise.

'To tell you that I'm sorry,' she yelled, standing on her tiptoes to bring her mouth closer to his ear. 'I won't stand in the way of what you want to do. I love you so much, and I was so frightened of losing you, but you were right—a life lived in fear is no life at—'

She didn't get any further because at that moment he captured the back of her head in one strong hand and brought his mouth down on hers, kissing her on and on as the cars streaked past on the track behind them, whipping her hair against his face. Her body arched against him, her bones melting as he held her in their own dark, sweet world. When the noise had died away again they pulled apart slowly, gazing at each other in stupefied wonder.

'What did you say?' Cristiano rasped, holding her face between his hands as her tears streamed over his fingers.

'I said I love you,' Kate sobbed. 'I want you—on any terms. Because I'd rather have five minutes of being loved by you than five hundred years of being loved by anyone else. So if you want to get into the car and go back out there, that's OK with me.'

'Kate...'

He kissed her again, with a tenderness that bordered on reverence this time. Kate smiled tremulously.

'But you'd better do it soon, because even you might struggle to make up time from an extended kissing stop in the middle of a race.'

He shook his head slowly. 'I'm not going anywhere. I've finally remembered what happened last time—in Monaco. But even before that I had realised anyway. I don't need this anymore. I don't need to risk my neck to feel alive, or win to prove that I'm something. Not if I have you and Alexander.'

She was dimly aware of cameras whirring at a distance, as the pit crew kept back the journalists who had gathered. Happiness was rising inside her like the sun, spilling warmth and shining light into the dark corners where fear had lurked for so long.

'You do. You will. Always.'

The sun dazzled her, making rainbows dance in the blur of tears as he stood in front of her. His face was pale, his narrow eyes black with fiercely restrained emotion. 'Does that mean that if I asked you to marry me again you might say yes this time?'

'Try,' she sobbed.

Gravely, he lowered himself down onto one knee, looking for all the world like some handsome crusader in a Pre-Raphaelite painting about to be knighted. Cars screamed past on the track behind them, but the noise that used to set her teeth on edge was now nothing more than a background symphony to Cristiano's voice.

'Kate Edwards,' he said, taking her hand, 'would you possibly be brave and foolish enough to risk joining your life to a dyslexic ex-racing driver who loves you more than he can ever say?' He looked up at her with a crooked, heartbreakingly sexy smile. 'Certainly on paper.'

Tipping back her head, Kate laughed, tears still cascading down her cheeks as she pulled him to his feet again. 'You know me—I thrive on risk. Bring on the challenge—and the happy ending.'

He caught hold of her waist and gathered her into his arms. 'Oh, no,' he said softly, his eyes gleaming as he bent his head to kiss her again. 'It's not the end. This is only just the beginning...'